Bruin Rawlins is a musk ox shifter who enjoys his job as a realtor since it allows him to meet so many new people. That increases his opportunity to find his mate—the other half of his soul. Imagine his surprise when it's not a client who turns out to be that special someone, but a beaten, battered human he finds in a home he's checking out. Giving in to his shifter instincts to care for his mate, Bruin takes the man home and, with the help of his brother, treats his injuries. When the human wakes, he panics and runs. To Bruin's embarrassment, it's his mammy who manages to calm him, taking him to call his family and giving Bruin a chance to learn his mate's name—Juan Ramirez. When Juan's relations arrive, other people are with them. Bruin learns that Juan already knows about shifters. Unfortunately, that doesn't mean he's ready to jump in and bond. Can Bruin earn Juan's trust while keeping him safe from whoever had hurt him?

The Realtor's Unexpected Find
Copyright © 2020 Charlie Richards
ISBN: 978-1-4874-3159-4
Cover art by Angela Waters

Published by eXtasy Books Inc or
Devine Destinies, an imprint of eXtasy Books Inc

Look for us online at:
www.eXtasybooks.com or www.devinedestinies.com

THE REALTOR'S UNEXPECTED FIND
KONTRA'S MENAGERIE BOOK TWENTY-NINE

BY

CHARLIE RICHARDS

DEDICATION

Nothing is more memorable than a smell.
~Unknown

CHAPTER ONE

Whistling along to the tune playing from his radio, Bruin Rawlins checked his GPS. He made the turn indicated and switched to singing. Bruin knew he couldn't carry a tune in a bucket, so he would have been embarrassed if anyone heard him, but there was just something about *Perry Como's It's a Good Day* that always put a smile on his face.

Bruin continued to grin as he switched back to whistling.

Yep, even I can't stand my singing.

Pulling up in front of the address indicated on his paperwork, Bruin picked up his metal clipboard. It was one of the thick kind that opened to store additional papers or small items. He opened it and tossed his truck keys inside before exiting his vehicle.

Walking to the sidewalk, Bruin took a few minutes to survey the neighborhood. He noticed most of the lawns appeared to have been mown recently and had nicely manicured hedges. A few had children's toys in the yard—tricycles, bikes, and plastic trucks. One house two doors down had sidewalk chalk marking up the driveway.

Bruin grinned. If the house behind him was as nice as the listing said, it would be perfect for the couple he intended to show it to that afternoon. As a realtor, Bruin always checked the home before taking a client there. He'd had one too many unpleasant surprises early on in his career, making a client walk away from not only the house, but him.

He'd learned from those experiences. It took more of his time, but he didn't mind. It was well worth it for the sterling reputation he'd eventually earned as well as all the word-of-mouth referrals that came with it.

For over a century and a half, Bruin had earned his living with his hands—first as a blacksmith, then in a variety of steel and other types of mills. As a musk ox shifter, he could live as long as five hundred years. He didn't want to do that without his mate—the other half of his soul. Working in mills and factories didn't give Bruin much of an opportunity to meet new people.

With that in mind, when Bruin and his family—his parents, four siblings, and a number of extended family members—had moved south to a different territory twelve years before, the identity he'd requested had given him a new focus. He'd learned to be a realtor. Bruin had always had a friendly personality with his herd-mates, while being more reserved with humans. He'd learned to adjust that.

His new occupation gave him the opportunity to meet plenty of people. He just knew he would run across his mate eventually. Until then, he enjoyed seeing different homes and making new friends.

Bruin gave the neighborhood one more cursory sweep, taking in the Halloween decorations in many of the yards. There were orange leaf bags painted with jack-o-lantern faces, skeletons, and witches. One house had a myriad of fake spider webs and spiders in their trees.

Grinning, Bruin headed toward the house. Just as he reached the door, his phone rang. He pulled it from his belt clip and checked the screen before answering it.

"Hey, Warren," Bruin greeted his older brother. "What's up?"

As Bruin had been speaking, he'd been checking his paperwork for the lockbox code.

"Hi, Bru," Warren replied. "I'm calling to make sure your

client showing this afternoon isn't going to interfere with Rochelle's birthday party."

While punching in the code, Bruin rolled his eyes. "As if
I'd ever miss my niece's birthday party." He pulled the
house's key from the now-open box and inserted it into the
lock. "Don't worry, Warren. I'll be there on time."

"Good. Because no way do I want to figure out a way to
tell my little girl that her favorite uncle . . ."

Bruin stepped into the house and immediately lost track of
what Warren was saying. The scent that hit his nostrils was
just too distracting. It contained an earthy fragrance mixed
with something sweet — like honeysuckle. Except, there was
an underlying hint of iron to it, too, as well as a bitterness that
set his musk ox on edge.

Goose bumps formed on his arms underneath his jacket,
and the hairs on his nape stood on end.

"Bruin? Bruin? Are you listening to me?"

"No," Bruin admitted when he finally registered Warren
calling his name. He had no idea how long he'd been standing
inside the foyer of the home, but now he started forward. His
need to identify the source of the confusing scent surged
through him. Part of it set his teeth on edge, even as arousal
began to burn through his system.

He didn't understand it one bit.

Evidently, something in Bruin's tone must have alerted
Warren. "What's going on, Bruin?" his older brother demanded. "What's wrong?"

As Warren was a damn dominant musk ox — and the head
enforcer for their herd — Bruin naturally followed his com-
mands . . . and answered his questions. "I don't know," he admitted. "There's a scent in here that's . . . I can't describe it."

"Are you at that house you plan to show your clients
later?"

"Yeah." Bruin tipped his head back and inhaled deeply.

"Well, isn't it sitting empty because it's on the market?" Warren started slowly. "Plenty of people could have been through it."

Bruin growled low in his throat. He didn't like Warren's logic, even if he was right. Tracking down and sniffing every person who'd toured the place would be a difficult, if not nearly impossible, task.

Except, as Bruin started up the stairs, the scent intensified. "Maybe, but—" Something told him he wouldn't have to do that. "This is too fresh. It's . . . current. *Here.*"

Reaching the top landing, Bruin took in the four closed doors. He knew from the listing information that three would lead to bedrooms and the fourth was a hall bathroom. Judging by the fact that the doors on the right were French doors, Bruin decided that was the master suite, which included an ensuite.

"Talk to me, Bruin," Warren urged. "What's going on?"

"I'm just exploring," Bruin replied absently as he sniffed around the space. He turned away from the French doors and headed toward the farthest one on the left. "Whoever this is, he was here recently."

Or he's still here.

Bruin didn't add that, since it was his own hope talking. Tucking his clipboard under his arm, he freed up a hand to reach for the knob. He paused an instant, feeling a shiver trickle up his spine, and he felt certain something important was about to happen.

His musk ox urged him to hurry up and open the door.

Obeying his animal, Bruin turned the knob. He pushed the door open, and a wall of the odor crashed over his senses. A growl he couldn't stop erupted from his throat as the smell of blood clogged his nostrils.

Stepping into the room, Bruin gasped, cutting off the noise. He almost whimpered instead. His heart tripped in his chest, and his body didn't seem to know how to respond to the sight before him—become aroused or become enraged.

Bruin dropped his clipboard in shock. The confusion to the smell in the house now made perfect sense. Lying on a thin mattress and tied to a crappy metal bedframe—nude, beaten, and bloody—was his mate.

"W-Warren," Bruin whispered, frozen to the spot, unable to tear his gaze away from the battered human on the bed. "I-I—"

"Talk to me, Bruin," Warren urged in a soothing croon. "Tell me what you see."

"My mate." Bruin barely managed to get the words out of his too-tight throat.

After a couple of seconds, Warren asked, "Did you just say that you see your mate?"

"Yeah."

"Uh, can you tell me a little more on that, Bru?"

Taking a deep breath, which caused his arousal to surge even as his gut churned that he was reacting like that when his mate was in such a state, Bruin managed to pull his head out of his ass. "Someone put one of those cheap metal bedframes in here with a thin mattress. He's on it. Tied to it." His words were barely a whisper, but he knew his brother's enhanced shifter hearing would easily allow him to make out his words. "He's been beaten, and he's naked, and there's blood . . . everywhere."

Bruin swept his gaze over the human's too-skinny frame, which spoke of malnourishment. He lay on his stomach with his head turned toward the door. His left eye appeared swollen shut, and there were a myriad of finger-like bruises around his wrists and ankles—as if someone squeezed way-too-hard when they shackled him. Bruises and dried blood littered nearly every part of his backside from what appeared to be a beating mixed with a caning.

He feared to see what the front of the man looked like.

"Bruin, you need to check for a pulse," Warren urged. "Check to see if he's . . . alive."

The hairs on his arms stood on end, but he did as his brother ordered. With a trembling hand, he reached out. After a few seconds of hesitation, he rested his fingertips gently on the man's neck, searching . . . searching . . .

Relief flooded Bruin when he felt the steady pulse beneath his fingertips. "I feel his pulse," he whispered. "It's steady. Does that mean this is all superficial?" Bruin swept his gaze over the man again. "How is this possible? How did it happen?"

"He needs help, Bruin," Warren reminded him, his tone gentle. "You need to call the cops."

Upon hearing Warren's advice, Bruin snarled. "No. I'll care for him," he stated gruffly. "I'll protect him." The need to comfort, care, and see his little mate returned to health surged through him like a tidal wave. "He's mine."

"Bruin, he's human," Warren reminded him. "You need to do it their way. Someone injured him. We need to involve the proper human authorities."

"No. I'll protect him," Bruin repeated adamantly. Then, referring to one of their younger brothers who worked as a nurse at a local clinic, he ordered, "Have Luke meet me at my house."

"Bruin —"

Ignoring Warren growling his name, his tone full of warning, Bruin disconnected the call. He leaned close to the human's swollen face and whispered, "I'll take care of you, my beautiful mate." Gently, Bruin swept the man's black hair away from his forehead and tucked it behind his ear, taking in his delicate features, acknowledging what the human reminded him of. "Take heart, my sprite. I'll be right back, and I'll get you out of here. You'll never be injured again." Unable to help himself, Bruin bussed a light kiss to the human's cheek. "I'll take care of everything."

Tearing himself away from the human was the most difficult thing Bruin had ever had to do. Except, he knew he couldn't carry a naked man from the home, no matter how much he wanted to do that right that instant. Bruin grabbed his clipboard from the floor as he rushed out of the room, his mind churning with ideas.

Bruin ignored his phone ringing, clipping it back to his belt, figuring it was Warren trying to change his mind about his actions. With his shifter instincts screaming at him to care for and defend his mate, that just wasn't going to happen. He needed to know his mate was safe, and being locked out of his hospital room because he wasn't a relation—hell, he didn't even know the man's name—wasn't an option.

After yanking his truck's back door open, Bruin grabbed the blanket folded on the floorboard. He closed the door before shaking out the blanket. Grains of sand tumbled from the fabric, since he'd used it for a picnic on the beach with his family two days before. Gratefulness filled Bruin that he'd forgotten to take it out. Even with a little sand, it was better than nothing.

Leaving the front passenger side door open, Bruin returned to the house. He placed the key back in the box, leaving that door open, too. Then he hustled to the bedroom, taking the steps two at a time.

Bruin lay the blanket on the floor, then turned his attention to the cuffs. They were of decent quality, he supposed, but they weren't anything a shifter couldn't break. Gripping the metal, he easily popped them open, one at a time.

Once his human was free, Bruin crooned into his ear as he slid his arms under him—one at his upper torso and the other at his thighs. He didn't know if the man could hear him or not, but he offered reassurances anyway as he moved him to the blanket. Then Bruin wrapped him up, tucking the blanket tightly around him, and picked him up again.

Carefully closing up the house before tucking his mate into the passenger seat of his pick-up, Bruin thought about the *Perry Como* song.

This is indeed a good day.

Bruin started his truck and took his mate home with him.

CHAPTER TWO

Juan Ramirez kept his breathing steady, even though it hurt. The tightness in his chest was the least of his worries. He figured Crespin had bruised or even cracked a rib or two the last time he'd worked over his chest.

He needed to know if Crespin was in the room before he risked cracking open his eyelids—if they weren't swollen shut—and looking around. Surely there was a way to escape. He wasn't certain he could last long enough against his half-brother for his friends to find him.

Thinking about the shifter motorcycle gang he'd been riding with gave him hope. In the past, no one would have been looking for him. His parents had died years ago, and his half-brother had dragged him halfway across Texas to join a different armadillo roll so he could force a mating on a woman named Maria—all in the name of power. He'd taken Juan along for the ride because he liked having someone under his thumb to clean his house and cook his food . . . and who he could occasionally beat on.

Asshole.

When Maria's brother came with a bunch of dominant shifters and took her away, Maria had offered Juan a place with them, too. While some of the guys had looked rough, there were a few smaller guys, too, as well as a couple of other humans. After living with Crespin, practically as the man's slave, for the last several years, Juan was willing to take the devil he didn't know.

Nothing could be as bad as Crespin, right?

Fortunately, the gang—led by a grizzly shifter named Kontra Belikov—had been fantastic. They'd created a new identity for him, had started tutoring him in stocks and investing, and had shared their clothes and money with him. Juan had even finally stopped looking like an emaciated skeleton.

And then Crespin snatched me while at a shopping center with others in the gang. How did he find me?

Juan hadn't asked, knowing the asshole didn't like questions. Instead, he'd listened to him rant and rave about losing status in his roll due to Kontra's interference. He wanted to know where Maria and his children were.

Juan had never opened his mouth, and he never would. As long as his pseudo-sister and his nieces and nephews were safe, it didn't matter what happened to him. No way would he condemn the only family that still cared for him to return to an abusive life with Crespin and his roll.

Returning to his own predicament, Juan realized he didn't hear anyone moving around the room or even breathing. He knew Crespin sometimes liked to sit in a chair and stare at him, waiting for him to wake up. Then he would start on the questions while beating him again.

Taking a chance, Juan eased open his eyelids. Well, his right one, anyway. His left remained stubbornly shut.

Great.

Still, Juan would take it.

Juan was still lying on his stomach, just as he'd been when Crespin had shackled him to the bed and left. Except, he saw that it wasn't the same bed. The one he lay on right then was much nicer. The room was also fully furnished with black furniture sporting chrome accents, giving it a modern masculine feel.

As Juan forced himself up onto an elbow, biting his lip to keep in his hiss, he realized that he wasn't shackled anymore, either. In fact, the cuts he'd procured on his wrists from trying to tug free had been bandaged. A glance over his shoulder told him his back and thighs had also been cleaned up and cared for.

Rolling to his side, Juan looked down his front. Once again, his wounds had been cleaned up and treated.

Confusion filled Juan, but it didn't last long. One of Crespin's threats replayed in his mind.

"You'll do as you're told, Juan, or I'll find another way to make you useful." Crespin's cold, brown-eyed gaze swept over Juan's body as he curled his lip. "I know a few guys who've asked for a chance at your skinny body." Smirking, Crespin had laughed cruelly. "Maybe I'll give them some time with you . . . for a price."

Crespin must have finally done it, and whoever intended to have his ass must not have wanted him bleeding all over the sheets. Or he wanted Juan healthy so he could take him whenever he wanted.

Fear permeated Juan, and he scrambled off the bed. He peered around the room, searching for a weapon . . . or an escape. To his left was a door to an ensuite bathroom. Two other doors were closed — a closet and the exit, perhaps. Continuing to turn, Juan spotted one more door on the other side of the bed. Judging by the curtains mostly covering it, it led to a balcony.

Creeping on silent feet, Juan crossed to it. He looked out . . . and didn't see a whole lot. It was a yard. The lawn showed signs of recent trimming, and a gazebo standing off to the right had been done up with Halloween decorations.

Juan shook his head in confusion. What kind of shifter who was friends with Crespin would put up decorations?

Deciding that was a puzzle easily left uncompleted, Juan looked at his nude form. He turned to the dressers, wondering if there was anything in them. Just as he was debating trying to silently search them, the soft creaking sound of footsteps climbing stairs reached Juan's ears. Someone was heading his way.

Decision made.

After all, if a human spotted Juan naked, they would offer help.

Hopefully.

Juan just had to get out of this shifter community—and he assumed he was in a shifter community because Crespin didn't like associating with humans. Surely he wouldn't sell him to a human, even for money. Anyway, Juan wasn't willing to stick around and find out.

Gripping the doorknob, Juan turned it. To his relief—and surprise—it gave way easily. Juan gritted his teeth against the pain as he tugged carefully, hoping the hinges wouldn't squeak.

They didn't.

Nice.

Juan slipped from the house onto the small deck. The warm, humid air of a coastal town wrapped around him, causing his skin to goose bump. Grateful for the current mild temperature, Juan hurried to the railing's edge.

Looking down, Juan calculated a way down to the lawn. He could think of only one. Conscious of his dangling bits, he swung his leg over the railing. Once he had both feet on the outside of the railing, he crouched. Ignoring the pain racking his body, Juan stuck out his right leg and felt with his toes.

Feeling the wood against his foot, Juan slowly walked his hands down the slat so he could move his second foot directly beneath his right. Then he eased as low as he could on the upright and moved his hands to the deck planking. After a glance down, he pushed away from the pylon with his feet while letting go with his hands.

With a jolt, Juan's feet hit the ground. He went with the momentum, allowing his knees to buckle. Tumbling backward onto his ass, he couldn't hold in his cry of pain as agony spiked through his body.

Tears formed in his eyes as black spots swam across his vision. He panted hard, trying to force his lungs to get enough air into him to catch his breath. Even as he screamed in his mind to move, he couldn't get his traumatized body to obey.

"My sprite?" a deep voice called from above. "Oh, sprite. Why did you do that?"

Juan jerked his gaze to the deck he'd just dropped from. Staring at him from over the railing was a mountain of a man—wide shoulders, thick limbs, with a bit of a pudgy middle. His bearded lips were curved into a frown, and his dark brows were furrowed.

For a second, Juan found himself attracted to the guy. Then he remembered who the man was friends with. Squashing any hint of desire, Juan finally managed to force himself to move.

Jumping to his feet—well, more of a lurch—Juan glanced around, picked a direction, and ran.

"Wait!" the man called.

Juan didn't listen. Sprinting around the side of the house, he quickly decided which way to go. He heard the sounds of children's laughter. Happy children meant nice people, right?

He could only hope.

Jogging across the street, Juan headed toward the noise. He passed one house, then a second, before spotting some people milling around behind the third. They were dressed casually, holding plates with cake on them while laughing and talking between bites. Beyond them, Juan could just make out the edge of a massive, pink, blow-up bouncy house castle.

A little girl's birthday party. Oh, god.

Juan froze.

What if they were human? Was he about to traumatize some little girl?

"Wait!" that deep voice called from behind him. "Little sprite, please stop."

After a glance over his shoulder and spotting the huge man lumbering toward him, Juan decided he didn't have a choice. He had to try. His freedom — and perhaps his life — depended on it.

Juan started toward the three that he could see — two women and a man — waving and shouting, "Help! Please, help?"

Their laughter immediately stopped, and their brows lifted, then furrowed as they looked beyond him. The older dark-haired woman handed her plate to the man. She took off her jacket and held it out to Juan.

"What's the matter, sweetie?" she asked.

That was a good sign.

Taking it, Juan wrapped it around his waist. "I'm so sorry to interrupt like this. I — " He paused, uncertain how to explain. He didn't know if these people were human or shifter, so he didn't know what he could share. Finally, Juan blurted out, "My half-brother kidnapped me and beat me, and I think he sold me to the man following me and — "

The woman immediately whipped her attention to his follower. "Bruin Wilfred Rawlins," she barked. Her expression turned fierce as she wrapped her arm around Juan in a hold that felt motherly and protective all at the same time. "Did you buy this young man like some kind of cattle?"

Juan tensed. "You know him?" He whispered the words, fear flooding him. Would she believe the man chasing him — Bruin — over himself?

Bruin lifted both hands, palms out. "No, Mammy," he claimed in his deep voice. "I didn't buy him from" — his brows furrowed as his focus shifted to Juan — "his half-brother?"

"Then where did this young man come from, Bruin?" she asked pointedly. "And how did you get him away from his half-brother?" Then she shifted her focus to Juan and gave him a sad smile. "Your half-brother sounds like a real piece of work."

When Bruin stopped before the group, Juan couldn't help but edge behind the woman, who was evidently Bruin's mother. She didn't look a day over forty, certainly far too young to have a son who appeared in his mid-thirties, but that was the way of shifters. Once they hit what human's would consider middle-age, their aging essentially stopped . . . for centuries.

So not fair.

Bruin sighed as he shoved his hands into his jeans pockets. "I found him in a house I was planning to show a client," he claimed, confusing Juan even further. "He was all alone and chained to a bed. I—" Appearing uncertain, Bruin shoved his fingers into his thick dark hair, tugging at it lightly. "He—I— I brought him home with me and asked Luke to tend his wounds. I went downstairs to get him some soup for when he woke, but when I got back to the room, he was—" Pausing, Bruin waved his hand in an absent manner.

"Already runnin'," Bruin's mammy finished for him with a nod and a sage look. "Of course. That makes total sense." She turned and smiled at Juan. "Please know you're totally safe here, sweetie." She waved her hand at Bruin. "Bruin really is like a big teddy bear, and sometimes he thinks with his heart instead of his head." Touching her own chest, she told him, "I'm his mammy, Nancy, but you can call me mammy." With an arm around Juan's waist, she refused to release him. "Let's get you in the house. I think Rylie's clothes will fit you." She pointed toward the backyard. "Bruin, go find Rylie, please, and ask him to get something comfortable for our new friend." Then she continued them both walking. "Is there anyone you need to call and let know you're here?"

Juan realized damn fast that Nancy had to be the matriarch of the family, pack, whatever they called it. He allowed her to guide him around to the front of the house. The promise of a phone and clothes couldn't be resisted.

Plus, it gave Juan a reprieve from the guy who was causing his body to give him mixed signals — arousal and fear.

CHAPTER THREE

Bruin realized his mate's first impression of him was . . . horrible. As he moved toward the backyard, he gave his mate one last lingering look. At least, he knew his human would be safe with his mammy.

As Bruin strode around the backyard — after all, the faster he found his nephew, Rylie, the faster he could return to his mate — he noticed Luke fall into step beside him. His younger brother smirked as he handed him Mammy's piece of cake. He took it with a sigh, then noticed not one bite had been taken out of it, yet.

Arching a brow at Luke, Bruin asked, "You think I'm supposed to sit around and eat cake while my confused mate is in there with Mammy?"

Luke barked a laugh as he shook his head. "Of course not, ya numpty." He waved at the plate. "Take the cake to your mate. In fact, grab a few things from the grill, too. Give him some choices. I bet he's hungry."

"Good idea," Bruin acknowledged. He appreciated that his family was trying to help.

His sister, Naomi, had fallen into step on the other side. "Your mate, huh?" She bumped her shoulder into his upper arm, which was as high as her six-foot frame could reach against his own six-foot-four. "He's cute."

"Get your own mate," Bruin growled with a scowl at her.

Naomi laughed as she rolled her eyes. "I was giving him and you a compliment, douche," she claimed with a smirk. "And he's totally not my type." With a wink, Naomi added,

17

"I like mine with big tits and a pussy."

"My ears are bleeding," Luke cried exaggeratedly, lifting his free hand to one ear. "La-la-la-la."

Laughing at their antics, Bruin realized he felt better, calmer, more clear-headed. He would get Rylie, take his mate some food and cake, and explain the situation to him. Then they could go on a date together, and he would woo his human while keeping him safe from his asshole half-brother.

With his plan in mind, Bruin spotted Rylie near the deck. The teenager had just started a growth spurt, so it wouldn't be long before the five-foot-nine fifteen-year-old wouldn't have been able to share clothes with his mate. As it was, Rylie's things would probably hang on his sprite's skinny frame.

I really need to find out his name.

"Hey, Rylie," Bruin called, jogging toward him. "I need a hand."

"Hi, Uncle Bruin," Rylie called with a grin. "I heard you found your mate. Congrats!" The youngster peered behind him. "Did you bring him with you?"

"Sort of. And thanks," Bruin hedged. "He's in with Mammy right now. He needs some clothes, and he's about your size. Can you run and get some sweats and maybe a soft sweatshirt or a long-sleeved t-shirt for him?"

Rylie nodded with a smile. "Sure thing." He set his plate of food on a nearby table and started jogging next door. "Be back in a jiffy!" Then the teenager picked up his pace.

Bruin turned his attention to the spread of food that had been prepared for Rochelle's birthday. As he started making up a plate, he glanced around for the lady of the hour. He spotted her playing in the bouncy castle, so he made a mental note to track her down later.

After piling two plates high with several pieces of pizza, a couple of hotdogs with everything, and an assortment of sides, he carefully balanced them and the cake plate and made his way inside. Fortunately, Warren appeared — with a stern pinch creasing his lips — to open the door for him. He ducked his head in submission, knowing he'd annoyed his older brother when he'd ignored him.

Still, Bruin wouldn't have changed anything. Well, maybe he would have made certain he was with his mate when he'd woken so that he could soothe his fears. Hearing his mother's voice to his right, Bruin realized they were in the family room, so he turned that way.

"Hi, Mammy," Bruin greeted, casting a tentative smile his sprite's way. "Rylie should be back shortly with clothes, and I have some food for you."

His mate sat curled up in a large recliner, his legs tucked under him. One of his mammy's quilts was wrapped around his body. He stared up at him with haunted brown eyes, but at least he met his gaze.

"Thank you," his human murmured.

His soft tenor went straight to Bruin's balls, but he did his best to ignore it. There would be no hanky-panky in the near future. While Luke had told him that his mate hadn't been violated when he'd been tied to that bed, he did have a couple of cracked ribs, more bruises than he wanted to count, and numerous welts cross-crossing his back and thighs.

Seeing him sitting there like that, Bruin couldn't imagine the pain he was in. Either that or he had a really high threshold for pain. Neither option made Bruin or his musk ox happy.

When it didn't seem that his mate was going to say anything else, Bruin cleared his throat. "Um, so . . . I didn't know what you liked." He eased closer and set the plates on the side table positioned between the pair of recliners. "There's other things out there, too," Bruin added as he watched his mate look over his offerings. "Or I can make up a dog any way you like."

Taking a chance, Bruin settled in the other recliner and rested his weight on the arm, leaning toward his human before placing a fork and knife next to the plate. "Plus, there's plenty to drink. Sodas, *Gatorade*s, water, beer, wine." Offering him a smile, he told him, "Or if you have a request, I'll try to fulfill it."

To Bruin's pleasure, his sprite picked up one of the three-meat pieces of pizza. There was a plain cheese on there, too, since some humans preferred a vegetarian diet. As a musk ox, he ate a lot more veggies than predator shifters, but he still enjoyed the occasional steak.

After chewing and swallowing, his mate licked his lips . . . which went straight to Bruin's dick. He had to straighten in his seat to find a slightly more comfortable position for his cock. When his mother cleared her throat, Bruin felt his cheeks heat.

Gods, getting hard around my mammy is so damn embarrassing.

Except, Bruin had seen his parents randy for each other on more than one occasion. He figured his father—Winston—would be joining them soon enough. It would take a little while to pry him away from the grill.

"Thank you for this," his mate murmured. "It's good."

"You're welcome," Bruin replied. Indicating the food, he asked, "May I join you?"

The man's gorgeous brown eyes widened, and he quickly nodded. "Of course." After clearing his throat, he added, "Um, thank you for not calling the cops." His cheeks darkened as he admitted, "I wouldn't have wanted them involved. It's family shit, and we'll handle it."

Bruin didn't like that claim, but he held his tongue. Instead, he picked up one of the hotdogs while asking, "Since we weren't officially introduced, I'm Bruin Rawlins. What's your name?"

Bruin didn't bother offering his hand. He'd seen his mate cringe away from him enough. Considering he was beaten by a family member, someone he should have been able to trust, his mate would need time to come to trust him.

His brows shot up his forehead as his cheeks took on a pinkish hue. He swallowed his bite of pizza before murmuring, "Um, sorry. I'm Juan Ramirez."

Smiling, Bruin told him, "It's very nice to meet you, Juan." As he lifted his dog to his lips, he added with a pained smile, "Although I truly wish it could have been under other circumstances."

Juan didn't respond other than by taking another bite of pizza.

"So, did you decide if you wanted a drink?" Bruin asked curiously between bites. "I'm in the mood for a beer, myself." With a wink, he added, "And I need to say hello to the birthday girl. That's my niece, Rochelle. She's turning six today."

Just then, the sound of the back door opening drew Bruin's attention, followed by Rylie calling, "Hey, Uncle Bruin? Where are you?"

"We're in here, Ry," Bruin called back. "Family room." Turning to Juan, he added, "And this is Rochelle's older brother, my nephew Rylie."

Rylie entered the room, a huge grin on his face. "Hey, Mammy. Uncle Bruin." Then he turned to Juan and opened a can of worms by saying, "Hi, Bruin's mate. Great to meet ya." He cut a glance toward Mammy as a sly smile curved his lips. Then Rylie turned back to Juan and teased, "Guess Uncle Bruin got a little excited, and your clothes paid the price, eh?"

As Juan's face took on a deeper shade of red, Rylie erupted into a fit of giggles.

Bruin growled, and he opened his mouth, ready to chasten his nephew.

His mammy beat him to it. "You have obviously been spending too much time with Marcus if you think it's okay to speak to your elders that way." With a warning look, she added, "Thank you for the clothes. When Juan is feeling better, we'll introduce him to everyone." Her dismissal was clear in her tone.

Rylie placed the bag of clothes on the coffee table as he swept his gaze over Juan again. He must have finally noticed his pale skin, pinched expression, and the way he clutched the blanket to him in discomfort. Lifting his hands, he offered an apology.

"I'm sorry. I wasn't thinking. You did have to see Uncle Luke, after all," Smiling faintly, Rylie added, "I hope you feel better."

With another grin, Rylie trotted from the room.

"I—"

Bruin paused, having no idea how to explain Rylie's comments without sharing shifters and mates. He just knew that Juan wasn't ready for that. His musk ox would simply have to be patient. Unfortunately, claiming their mate wasn't in the cards anytime soon.

"Does everyone know how you found me?" Juan asked, frowning at his pizza crust before shoving a bite of it into his mouth.

"No. Absolutely not," Bruin replied, pleased to be able to put his sprite at ease about that. "My brother Warren was on the phone with me when I found you. My other brother Luke tended your wounds." Then Bruin indicated Mammy. "And Mammy is our matriarch, so of course, I told her. Everyone else"—he tried to decide how to finish and continued lamely—"thinks I brought home . . ."

"Your injured mate," Juan finished for him.

Before Bruin could do much more than nod as he tried to decide what Juan was thinking about the word use, the roar of several motorcycle engines reached his ears. Cocking his head, he arched one brow as he focused on his mammy.

His mammy hummed, having obviously heard it, too. With

a smile at Juan, she rose to her feet. "You said your family rides motorcycles?" After Juan nodded, she picked up the bag of clothes and handed it to him. "Get dressed. They're here." Then she beckoned to Bruin. "Come. We'll make certain no one enters while he dresses."

Bruin didn't want to leave his injured mate, but he couldn't disobey his mammy, either. While they called her the family matriarch when speaking to humans, she was their herd alpha. That meant when she said move, Bruin obeyed.

Once they were out of the family room, she pointed to the front door. "Go to the door and meet them in the driveway," she instructed. "They should be told not to hug him too tightly."

Nodding, Bruin hurried to the front. He didn't want his mate injured further, so it was wise advice. Spotting half a dozen motorcycles, several containing two men, while a fourth had a woman on the back, Bruin waved.

As they stopped and parked nearby, Bruin's musk ox rumbled uneasily in his mind. When they swung from their bikes, removed their helmets, and turned to face him, he understood why. Their scents were heavily laden with predator shifters . . . as well as others.

Bruin barely managed to keep from gaping as he asked, "You're Juan's family?" He shook his head. "But you're shifters."

The biggest man, who sported silvery flecks in his dark-brown hair, stuck out his hand. "I'm Alpha Kontra Belikov, grizzly shifter."

After Bruin shook and released, Kontra pointed at the woman. "This is Maria Ramirez, Juan's ex-sister-in-law, but more of a true sister than his half-brother ever was." Then Kontra crossed his arms over his chest. "Tell me everything."

Feeling the power radiating off the bear, Bruin had no choice but to obey.

Chapter Four

Mate. The man – Bruin – is claiming me as his mate. Juan had spent his entire life around shifters, so he knew what that meant to them. As he scrambled to get dressed as swiftly as possible, he turned that revelation over in his mind. After being brutalized by Crespin for years, Juan didn't know if he wanted to tie himself to one for . . . well, centuries.

Except, Juan knew not all shifters were like that. There were plenty of kind and caring ones . . . like his pseudo-sister, Maria. Plus, there was Kontra and his gang. They'd taken him in even though he was just some random human.

If a shifter met his fated mate, they claimed to plan to care for and please that person for the rest of their lives. He or she would dote on the person, making them the center of their lives. Besides wanting their mate happy, a shifter wouldn't even look at another person. They were completely devoted.

Juan just wasn't certain if he believed Bruin's claims. After all, he hadn't actually said it to him. He'd told his family, though, and wouldn't they call him on a lie if he wasn't being truthful?

Maybe Bruin's people chose mates like Crespin's friends did.

Kontra would be able to help him figure that out. If Bruin was a good man, surely he would make a good mate. While Juan didn't feel comfortable jumping into anything with the near-stranger, he recognized his attraction to him. Maybe he should get to know him a little before making a decision.

I certainly don't want to allow Crespin's treatment of me to make me lose the chance at finding a partnership like the guys in the gang have with their mates.

Juan decided to ask for their help. He needed guidance from shifters he trusted. With that in mind, he finished tugging on the thick socks the teenager had brought, then folded the blanket and placed it over the back of the sofa.

Then Juan moved toward the doorway, eager to see his friends. Judging by the number of motorcycle engines, plenty of them had dropped everything to come to him when he'd called. They'd told him they'd been looking for him for three days.

Gods, three more days stolen by Crespin.

Pushing thoughts of that asshole out of his mind—Juan knew he would have to deal with talking about him soon enough—he decided to find his friends. He could use a supportive hug right about then, and Yuma and Caleb gave the best hugs. Even Alpha Kontra's hugs were wonderful, blanketing him in a sense of safety he hadn't experienced since before his parents died.

When Juan exited the family room, he spotted Nancy standing near a set of sliding glass doors. She was speaking with a big male who looked similar to Bruin, except he didn't have the warm brown eyes. His gaze was cooler, holding more intensity.

Looking over Nancy's shoulder, the man pinned Juan with that gaze, and a shiver worked down Juan's spine.

Juan took a step backward on instinct.

The man's eyebrows furrowed just a bit. Then his expression softened, and his lips curved in a fraction of a smile. He squeezed Nancy's shoulder and indicated with his chin.

Nancy turned and beamed at him even as she swept her gaze over his body, as if assessing the fit of his clothes. "There you are, sweetie." She moved around the table toward him. With a wave of her hand, Nancy indicated the big man behind her. "This is my eldest son, Warren. If you ever need anything and can't find myself or Bruin, he'll be able to help you."

While Juan nodded, murmuring, "Nice to meet you," he didn't think he would ever be brave enough to approach the intense man.

Bruin had said that Nancy was their matriarch. In a shifter pack, that was another word for alpha. Her mate would be the alpha-mate. Their sons could very well be a beta or enforcers.

Considering Warren's intensity, Juan would peg him as an enforcer of some level.

Perhaps catching on to Juan's unease—or maybe scenting it—Nancy patted her son on his shoulder. "Let's go see Juan's family, hmm?" She rounded the table, crossing to him. Resting her hand in the middle of Juan's back, Nancy asked, "So, who should we be expecting, sweetie?" With a wink, she added, "That seemed to be quite the number of motorcycle engines."

Juan didn't know how to answer that without giving away that he knew about shifters . . . or that he believed they were shifters, too. A human didn't make those kinds of statements. Finally, he decided to give a round-about response.

"They told me they've been searching for me for three days." Grimacing, Juan hated that he'd been in Crespin's clutches for so long . . . again. Something else they said drew a smile to his lips. "They said some of the guys were drawing straws to see who could come since they didn't want to overwhelm the neighborhood with the prospect of an invading motorcycle gang."

Even as Nancy laughed, she opened the front door. When they stepped onto the front porch, she only managed two steps before she paused and sniffed. Her eyes widened, and she turned toward Warren. "Call your father and your Uncle Ryzer, please."

Sighing, Juan moved away from her and limped down the porch stairs. He knew what that order was about. While leading him into the family room and wrapping him in her quilt, Nancy had yammered on about her family—who was who and such.

Juan had guessed she'd been doing it to help keep him calm. Now, he valued the information. Warren's father was Winston. What position he actually held in their pack was still up in the air in Juan's mind. Ryzer was Nancy's younger brother. That could put him as the beta or an enforcer.

"Are you certain these are your family and friends, Juan?" Nancy asked, touching his arm and stopping his forward momentum. She leaned close while cradling his neck in a warm hold. Her dark-brown eyes—so similar to Bruin's—held a wealth of concern. "If you're worried they will harm us if you don't go with them, please don't. We can handle them."

Shocked, Juan gaped. He could count on one hand how many people had taken a stand to help him, and both of them were standing in the driveway waiting for him—Maria and Kontra. While Juan believed many of Kontra's people would have done the same without prompting, rescuing him had been done on the bear's orders, so he lumped them all together.

"They're not like that, Alpha Nancy," Juan murmured, peering at her from beneath his lashes. "They're the good guys. I promise."

Nancy cocked her head as she lifted her brows. "You know about us."

Juan nodded once. Figuring it was all going to come out anyway, he admitted, "The man I called my father, Dale, was an armadillo shifter. My mother was human, but they weren't fated mates. During a turbulent time in their . . . marriage, my mom had an affair . . . with another human, and I was the result." Smiling as he thought of the man he'd called his father,

Juan admitted, "Even though I wasn't his blood and wasn't even a shifter, my father, Dale, still claimed me as his son." Lowering his voice, he whispered, "He was a good dad. I don't know how Crespin turned out the way he did, since Crespin is a bullying asshole, and my dad was amazing."

"Sometimes, the apple rolls far, *far* from the tree," Nancy stated sagely as she straightened. "Let's go meet your friends."

As Nancy once again began heading toward the group, Warren fell into step, flanking her. Bruin already stood before Kontra, murmuring something. When he spotted his family and Juan, his gaze focused on him, banked hunger in his brown eyes.

Juan shivered and wrapped his arms around himself. He knew it wasn't revulsion, though. His gut had warmed, after all. Having never been with anyone—Crespin kept way too close an eye on him for that kind of thing—Juan wasn't certain how to process what he was feeling.

The mate-pull, perhaps.

Bruin looked away, a tick forming in his jaw. Sam—Kontra's beta, a Texas longhorn bull shifter—gripped his shoulder and squeezed in a way that appeared commiserating. At the same time, Payson—a hyena shifter and gang enforcer—leaned close, stood on his toes, and whispered something into Bruin's ear. The guy's head immediately whipped around to stare at him, his lips parting and shock evident on his features. When Sam cuffed Payson on the back of his head, the hyena shifter cackled.

Before Juan could even hazard a guess at what Payson had said—probably something sex-related—Maria squealed. She ducked between a couple of the men and sprinted toward him. Just before she reached Juan, she slowed, embracing him carefully.

"We were so worried about you, Juan," Maria murmured into his ear. "I'm so sorry we lost you in the crowd. It will never happen again." She gripped his upper arms and leaned away, inspecting his face while nibbling her bottom lip. Maria's expression turned pained. "With your face looking like that, I'm afraid to see the rest of you. I'm so sorry."

Considering the way Maria had hugged him and how she spoke, Juan figured Bruin had told them about his injuries.

Probably for the best.

Juan pulled Maria in tight again. "Stop apologizing," he ordered. "None of this was your fault. It's never been your fault." Cradling her neck, Juan met her gaze. "Believe that. Okay?"

Even as Maria nodded, she nibbled her bottom lip, telling Juan she didn't completely agree with him. Before he could offer more words of comfort, she whispered, "Was it really Crespin?" Maria glanced over her shoulder at Bruin. "He said you told his mammy that you were kidnapped and beaten by your half-brother, but he couldn't confirm a name." Fear filled her brown eyes as she refocused on Juan. "Is Crespin really in town?"

Juan hated seeing the fear in Maria's eyes, but he would never lie to her. "It was him," he told her. Then he raised his voice and caught Kontra's eye. "Crespin kept asking me where his mate and cubs were, but I wouldn't tell him anything."

Feeling Maria tremble in his arms and hearing her whimper, Juan tightened his hold.

Kontra stepped forward and wrapped them both up. "Easy, Maria," he rumbled as he rubbed up and down her back with one huge hand. "Your cubs are safe. You'll never lose them." He swept the hand up her back to cradle her nape in a reassuring alpha-hold. "You and your cubs are part of my gang now. We take care of our own. Sam has already contacted Mutegi, and security at the hotel is being tightened." A low growl vibrated from the huge male. "I almost hope he tries to swing by, so we can deal with him . . . permanently."

Maria sniffed before lifting her head from Juan's chest. She turned a pained smile Kontra's way. "I just want him to leave us alone."

"We'll make sure it happens," Kontra assured. Then he turned his focus to Juan. His smile softened. "So . . . you met your fated mate. Congratulations." Before Juan could come up with a response, Kontra continued, "Now what do you want to do about it?"

Juan opened his mouth, then closed it again.

Well, damn. Isn't that the question?

CHAPTER FIVE

"Where are you going on your date tonight?" Luke asked from where he leaned against the doorframe with one shoulder. He eyed the shirt Bruin held in his hand. "Is that what you're wearing?"

Holding up the long-sleeve, button-down on the hanger, Bruin eyed the dark-blue shirt. "What's wrong with it?" Then he refocused on Luke. "And it's not a date. It's a bunch of guys hanging out and barbequing."

Luke scoffed as he closed the distance between them. "It's not a date for most of the guys, sure," he stated as he plucked the shirt from his grip. He tossed it on the bed, then headed to Bruin's closet. As Luke opened the door, he peered over his shoulder and told him, "You, however, are on a date."

Bruin growled as he followed his brother to his closet. "How do you figure?"

Scoffing, Luke rolled his eyes as he began rummaging through Bruin's clothes. "Juan didn't reject you. Remember that," Luke told him as he pulled a shirt off the rack. Shaking his head, he put it back and kept looking, while saying, "He was just attacked by his sadistic brother, who's been torment-ing him for years. He needed a little time with people he trusted." Taking a deep-green polo shirt off the rack, Luke turned and faced him, his smile holding a hint of understand-ing. "I get you wanted the mate-bond to instantly make that you, but that's not how it works." Then Luke held out his shirt. "Wear this with"—he crossed to Bruin's dresser and pulled out a pair of jeans, which he tossed on his bed—

"those."

"How do you figure?" Bruin crossed his arms over his chest.

Luke scoffed. "The jeans make your ass look good, and the polo shirt will accentuate the hue of your medium-brown skin." Shaking his head, he scowled at him. "How do you call yourself a gay man?"

Scowling at his brother, Bruin pointed at the jeans. "They're a size too small and make my gut look huge." Then he indicated the polo shirt. "And that clings, which will make it even worse." Then Bruin added, "And I was talking about the date thing."

"He asked to see you, didn't he?" Luke pointed out. "He's just not ready to be alone with you. This is a date," he insisted. "You're getting together in an environment your mate finds safe. That way, you can find out more about each other. It's a date." Then Luke pointed at the clothes again. "And we're musk ox shifters. We're not buff, but we don't have a gut. We have a bit of a paunch." As if to emphasize his point, Luke lifted his shirt to reveal his own soft middle. Poking it, it didn't move. "A gut jiggles. Does yours jiggle?"

Bruin felt his face heat, unable to believe he was discussing something so asinine with his brother. "Fine. No."

"Really?" Luke released his shirt, then pointed at Bruin's belly. "Let's see. We should check."

"Not a chance," Bruin snarled, snatching up the shirt. Anything to make his brother shut up. "What are you doing here again? Other than bothering me, of course?"

In truth, Bruin actually appreciated Luke dropping by. His brother, so devoted and serious when it came to his studies and work as a nurse, was actually pretty silly. His jokes had relieved the tension during many a stressful moment . . . and occasionally got him into trouble.

"Oh, I came to tell you good luck from everyone in the family," Luke replied with a wide grin. Nodding, he pointed at the polo shirt Bruin had just slipped on. "Yep. That's a good choice." He picked up the jeans. "Now these."

Rolling his eyes, Bruin shoved the sweatpants he'd donned after his shower down and off his legs. As a shifter, nudity didn't bother most of them much. He and his brothers had seen each other in the buff more times than he could count.

Bruin took the jeans and slid his legs in. With a slight wiggle, he got the too-tight jeans up his hips. After buttoning them, Bruin felt restricted in his thighs and ass.

"See?" Bruin turned to his brother, then did a half-squat before standing again. "Too tight. How am I supposed to sit down comfortably?"

Luke sighed deeply, as if the weight of the world was upon his shoulders. "That's the style of those jeans," his brother told him with a shake of his head. "There's a little spandex in them, so they stretch." Reaching out, Luke slid his fingers into the waistband near Bruin's hip and tugged lightly, proving there was indeed a little room there. "The waist fits just right. It doesn't make your belly look any bigger. In fact, because it accentuates your thighs and ass, it actually draws attention away from the fact that your frame isn't ripped like some of those guys Juan is staying with." As if a lightbulb had turned on in his head, Luke stepped back and crossed his arms over his chest. "Is that what this is about? They're predator shifters. They're built differently naturally." Then he shrugged. "Besides, Juan is your mate. That's not gonna matter to him."

Bruin winced upon hearing Luke so succinctly state his fears. To his ears, they sounded stupid. He would never tell his brother, but the man was completely right.

Instead, Bruin took a deep breath and nodded. "Of course. Thank you." He turned and stared at himself in the full-length mirror attached to the back of his closet door. Turning, he eyed his ass and thighs. "Huh. I guess you're right."

His ass and thighs did look fantastic in the jeans.

"Of course I am," Luke stated, sounding smug. Then he clapped his hands. "Oh, another reason I'm here. Mammy wants information on Juan's half-brother." He began ticking off on his fingers. "Full name. Shifter species. Pack location. Height and looks, although a picture would be better." With a wink, Luke told him, "She's going to put Link on it."

Bruin grinned broadly. "If anyone can find anything, Link can."

Link was a computer nerd inside and out, even though he looked like a military survivalist. For some reason, he had the smallest gut of them all, even though he was taller than Bruin by an inch. His youngest brother shaved his head while sporting a thick beard, and even though he stayed inside on his computers most of the day, he still had a natural tan.

"That would definitely give me some peace of mind," Bruin admitted, rubbing the back of his neck. "Since Link works for the Shifter Council as head of their cybersecurity team, he has access to a lot of information."

Link's job offer was one of the reasons his herd had chosen to move to the outskirts of Savannah when they'd needed to relocate a couple of decades before.

"Exactly," Luke replied with a grin. "Oh, and I left something for you in the foyer. You better get out of here if you plan to be on time."

Bruin nodded. "Yeah, I'm leaving."

Eagerness replacing his concern from before, Bruin headed to the foyer. He sat on the boot box near the door and pulled on a pair of nice hiking boots. Standing, Bruin grabbed a jacket out of the closet and slipped it on.

Then Bruin focused on Luke, who'd picked up the paper bag that had previously been sitting on the box. From within, he pulled a bouquet of roses. "This is for you to give your mate," Luke told him seriously. Then he hefted the bag he still carried. "The other item in here is a bottle of *Crown Royal.* That's a gift from Mammy to Alpha Kontra, to garner good-will between our herds."

Bruin took the paper bag first and rolled down the top so it was closed. "Are you sure about giving a guy flowers?" he asked as he tentatively reached for the bouquet. "It is beauti-ful."

"From looking at your mate, I think he deserves a little pampering," Luke said, his tone uncharacteristically serious. "I bet he's never received a gift from a prospective lover be-fore, so even if he's not a flower kind of guy, he'll still appre-ciate them."

Having gotten the same vibe from Juan, Bruin nodded be-fore sniffing the flowers. "Thanks." He gave Luke a grateful smile, since he would never have thought of it. "My family is the best."

Luke grinned broadly. "That we are." He picked up Bruin's keys from the candy dish on the small table beside the door. "Go get'em, tiger."

Chuckling, Bruin shifted the bouquet into the crook of his elbow of the arm holding the bag. Then he took his keys. He followed Luke when his brother opened the door and led the way around to the garage.

With a few more words of advice and encouragement, Luke waved, and Bruin started on his way to his date.

As Bruin drove, his excitement turned to uneasy nerves. He did his best to quell them, but without Luke uttering en-couragement in his ear, it was tough. His happy-go-lucky brother had obviously been teasing and annoying him to dis-tract him.

Damn. How does he know to do that?

Bruin glanced at his GPS and followed the robotic voice to-ward the hotel the group was staying at. Instead of fixating on the fact that his mate had left him to go be with family and friends, he thought about his little mate's sweet, tentative smile and his sparkling brown eyes. He knew he could get lost in Juan's gaze, and he would already do anything to see that look on his human's face over and over.

Once Bruin reached the hotel, he parked his truck and slipped out. He rounded his vehicle and paused at the passenger side door. From the floorboard, Bruin retrieved the bouquet, having placed it there earlier so it didn't slide around and crush any of the flowers.

After giving it a quick inspection and finding it still perfect, Bruin grabbed the paper bag, locked up his truck, and headed into the hotel. He knew from Juan's texts the prior evening—after his buddies had replaced his cell phone for him—that his gang had leased out the entire bar and grill area. They'd told the hotel concierge it was for a double baby shower for Maria. It included her six-month-old baby boy—Jonah—and her unborn babe.

From what Bruin had heard, many others had been invited, too, including some councilmen and their enforcers.

Good thing my brother is on the cyber squad. I should know most of them at least by sight.

Squaring his shoulders, Bruin paused in the lobby. He spotted the sign indicating the baby shower and followed the arrow, which said head left. Another pointed down another hallway that ended with a door opening up onto an expansive patio, bar, and pool area.

Dozens of men, and a few women, milled around the space.

Bruin swept his gaze over everyone, relieved that he'd gone with Luke's clothing choices. His nice polo and high-end jeans fit in pretty well with the crowd. A couple of men even wore sports coats.

"Hey, you're Bruin, right?"

Turning his attention to the left, Bruin realized he'd been

standing in the doorway long enough for someone to approach him. He took in the short, slender male who sported black hair fixed in a spiky do, and the tips were frosted white. His brown eyes twinkled with warmth.

Bruin wasn't entirely certain what the man was from his scent, but it was mixed with a human's, telling him he was mated. Getting his head out of his ass, he nodded. "I am." He shifted the flowers so that he could hold out his hand. "Bruin Rawlins," he stated unnecessarily.

The man took his hand and grinned. "I'm Yuma Batacan. Nice to meet you." After releasing him, he eyed what he carried. "Since you know this isn't really a baby shower, I'm assuming at least one of those items is for Juan." With a wink, Yuma placed his hand in the crook of Bruin's elbow. "Come on, handsome. I'll take you to him."

Relief filled him that he wouldn't have to wade through the throng alone. "Thank you."

CHAPTER SIX

Juan stuck close to Yuma's human mate, Hunter, as well as Lamar—a peacock shifter—and his human mate, Rueben. Enforcer Mutegi with his human, Ben, were also nearby, as were the python shifter, Eli, and his wolf shifter mate, Sam. Of course, those last two were probably there to keep an eye on Juan and make certain he didn't over-exert himself.

Many people had exclaimed over Juan's swollen eye, and he'd glossed over the situation by saying he had a run-in with his half-brother. That way, word of Crespin's misdeeds could be discreetly circulated through the shifter world. Due to the fact that Crespin was an armadillo shifter and he'd attacked a human, he was now a wanted man.

Even though Juan was technically family, attacking a human was still against shifter law. The only time that didn't apply was if the human threatened the shifter, and it was self-defense. Juan could easily prove that wasn't the case, since shifters could scent lies.

One question and answer session was all it took to prove that Crespin had been in the wrong.

Juan wished he'd known about that law years before. Of course, he didn't think he would have been able to contact the Shifter Council while in Alpha Alberto's territory. Juan absently wondered why Crespin had left the alpha and his roll.

Or is Alpha Alberto nearby, too?

Flinching at that idea, Juan desperately hoped that wasn't the case.

"Hey, what has you frowning so much, Little Bit?" Rueben

asked, reaching over and squeezing his knee lightly. "Are you in pain?"

That question immediately drew Eli's attention. "Do you need to take something?" He glanced at his phone, probably checking the time. "It has been four hours since you took the *Tylenol*. I can get you an *ibuprofen*."

Juan knew that what the doctor was offering wasn't the standard two hundred milligram tablets. He had access to eight hundred ones. Except, Juan had been injured so many times, he hardly noticed the pain.

Shaking his head, Juan smiled at Eli. "I'm good. Thanks, though." Then he turned to Rueben and patted his hand. "No, I was just lost in my head. Thinking about my old alpha and my brother and —"

"Say no more," Rueben stated, cutting him off. "How about something to take your mind off all that?"

Squinting at a Rueben, who waggled his eyebrows, Juan asked warily, "Like what?"

Ruben laughed and tipped his chin toward the left. "Like your mate?"

Juan's heart sped up as he peered where Rueben indicated. There was Bruin, being led toward them by Yuma. His new friend had assured him that he would keep an eye out for the shifter, since wandering around would be too painful for Juan.

"Oh," Juan whispered, unable to tear his gaze away from Bruin. "Wow."

To Juan, Bruin looked fantastic. His thickly muscled legs were showcased in a pair of dark, form-fitting jeans. He had an open jacket over a green polo shirt, but even covered that way, Juan found his broad shoulders enticing.

"Mmmm," Adam hummed, leaning over Juan's shoulder and announcing his arrival. "Looks like Juan appreciates something he sees." Teasing, the white tiger shifter continued,

"Whatever could that be?"

Juan couldn't tear his gaze away from Bruin as he mumbled, "Ummm . . . no idea."

Several chuckles sounded around him. Someone patted him on his back. Adam's mate—the moose shifter, Noah—told him, "Being fixated on your mate is normal." Then he lowered his head so he could whisper into his ear, "Remember, Bruin is a shifter, and from what I've heard through the grapevine, a good man. He'll want you happy, so be honest about what you need. Okay?"

While Juan had figured he and Bruin would be the gossip of the gang, hearing confirmation finally pulled his attention away from his approaching mate—who'd been stopped by Alpha Kontra. "What do you mean?" Juan asked, tensing.

"I mean, if you need time, be honest." Noah grimaced, adding, "He won't push you, but also try not to say anything that would make it seem like you're rejecting him." Squeezing Juan's shoulder, Noah warned him, "That would really hurt him."

From the corner of his eye, Juan noticed Bruin give the alpha a paper bag, and he found his attention back on them. The alpha unfolded the top and looked inside. A grin immediately crossed his goateed lips, and he focused the look on Bruin. The alpha clapped him on the shoulder and thanked him.

Bruin ducked his head, his cheeks darkening a smidge. Then Alpha Kontra released him, said a few more things that Juan couldn't read on his lips, and headed in another direction. When Bruin turned to again walk toward Juan, their gazes clashed.

Even from a distance, Juan saw the way Bruin's nostrils flared and the heat that flashed in his dark eyes. He licked his lips, then gave in to Yuma's urging to get him moving again. A determined expression fell over his features as he picked up his pace, causing excitement and unease to churn in Juan's gut in equal measure.

Juan knew that he needed to take Noah's advice. He would have to be honest . . . about everything—from his fears to his inexperience. If Bruin wanted a life with him, it wouldn't be easy.

"You're right," Juan whispered, patting Noah's hand. Glancing around, he saw his new friends were focused on him. "Thanks, everyone."

As Juan went to stand so he could meet Bruin, his mate hurried his last few steps. "Please, don't get up for me, my sprite," Bruin urged, then dropped to one knee before him. "It's good to see you. These are for you."

Glancing between the flowers and Bruin's earnest expression, Juan nibbled his bottom lip. He took the flowers, peering at them as pleasure filled him. The bouquet held probably a dozen roses mixed with baby's breath and a couple other types of blooms that Juan didn't recognize.

Juan couldn't resist and lifted them to his nose. Inhaling deeply, he enjoyed the sweet, floral scent. When he refocused on Bruin, the big man's lips were curved into a pleased smile.

"No one's ever brought me flowers before," Juan admitted. "Thank you." After another glance at them, he peered at Bruin shyly from beneath his lashes. "They're lovely."

"I'm glad you like them," Bruin rumbled softly. Reaching out, he touched his fingertips to Juan's knee, but his gaze was roving over Juan's face. "How are you feeling, my sprite?"

"I'm okay," Juan replied. Moving his free hand slowly, he tentatively set his hand over Bruin's fingers. "Thanks to you."

Bruin turned his hand and gently threaded his fingers with Juan's. "I wish I could have found you sooner." Sadness and anger flickered across his face before a smile curved his lips again. "But you're safe now, and I know I'm not the only one that will make certain you stay that way."

Juan returned Bruin's smile. "Thank you." Then he sighed,

squeezing the big man's fingers. "Will you sit with me so we can, um, get to know each other?"

Nodding, Bruin told him, "I'd like that."

"Have my chair, man," Rueben offered, jumping to his feet. "I'm ready for a refill, anyway." He held up his empty beer bottle. "Either of you want anything?"

"Or food?" Lamar offered. "I smell the grill being fired up, so something should be available soon."

Bruin rose. "Thank you." He eased onto Rueben's chair, never letting go of Juan's hand. "I'll take a glass of whatever shiraz is handy. Or a cab is fine, too." Then Bruin focused on Juan. "What about you, my sweet? A drink?" His brows furrowed as he asked, "Or are you on meds where you shouldn't have alcohol? I can have a soda with you if you'd prefer."

Juan couldn't help but smile upon hearing Bruin's worried rambling. Squeezing the large, kind man's fingers, he told him, "I'm not on any meds that would be dangerous with a drink or two." Focusing on Rueben, he asked, "If there's a good white wine back there, I'll take a glass."

"You know there will be," Lamar stated with a lift of his chin. "I don't buy cheap wine."

Remembering that white wine was Lamar's alcohol of choice, Juan nodded. He barely managed to keep a straight face. He'd come to realize Lamar could be a bit of a snob and neat freak about certain things. Watching him with Rueben, who was rough and tumble and didn't mind getting dirty, he found their dynamic entertaining at times.

Somehow though, the pair worked.

"Thanks, Lamar," Juan replied instead. "I'm not ready for food, yet, though." Turning his attention back to Bruin, he told him, "Please don't think you have to wait for me to eat in order for you to do so. I know shifters have much larger appetites than humans do."

For some reason, Bruin glanced at his stomach, then away,

biting his lower lip.

Juan followed his gaze — first, to the man's thick waist with a little bit of bulge, then as he looked at Adam and Eli and a few other shifters. That, in conjunction with what he'd said, made him realize something. The big man was a little self-conscious about his shape around all these ripped shifters.

Huh.

Never in a million years would Juan have thought a shifter could have body hang-ups. After all, they got naked with each other on a regular basis. As it was, Juan had mostly been around armadillo shifters until recently, and most of them had a little pudge, although not as much as Bruin seemed to have. Juan had always wished his skinny frame had more meat on it, but it didn't matter how much or what he'd eaten growing up. He just had one of those metabolisms that processed everything swiftly.

Juan knew many wished for that, so he'd stopped trying.

It looks like we both have a few things to work through.

While Juan was pleased to discover he wasn't the only one with issues, he didn't like the uncertainty clouding Bruin's eyes. Releasing the other man's fingers drew the shifter's attention back to him. Seeing the questioning look there, Juan took a chance.

Girding up his courage, Juan slowly stretched his hand toward Bruin's face. "I've never been able to grow facial hair," he whispered a second before he touched Bruin's closely shorn goatee hairs. "It's softer than I would have imagined."

Bruin's nostrils flared, and his lips parted as he gasped softly. Holding Juan's gaze, he swallowed hard enough to cause his Adam's apple to bob. He seemed to be thinking quickly, trying to decide how to answer.

Liking that expression on Bruin much better, Juan decided to continue with, "I like big frames, Bruin." Then he couldn't stop himself from furrowing his brows. "On nice men, anyway. Like Kontra and Adam and . . . you." Sweeping his gaze slowly over Bruin's form, Juan felt heat creep up his neck and into his cheeks. He'd never been so bold, and it felt good to be able to express himself, even if it made him a tad uncomfortable, too . . . in his jeans. Dragging his focus back to Bruin's deep, dark eyes, Juan whispered, "I know being held in your arms would make me feel safe. That's perfect for me, because I get scared a lot."

"Oh, my sprite," Bruin murmured roughly. Lifting his hand, he cupped Juan's hand against his face and nuzzled against it. "I will do everything I can to chase away any fear you face."

Upon hearing that, Juan felt his heart speed up in his chest. "What if I'm afraid of sex?"

CHAPTER SEVEN

Bruin closed his eyes and nuzzled into Juan's touch a little more. As much as he loved his mate opening up to him, he wished they weren't having a discussion about sex in the middle of a bunch of guys he didn't know. Truthfully, Bruin didn't want a sex discussion with his mate in front of people he *did* know, either.

But Juan is choosing to open up now, which means he's comfortable with these men.

Sucking it up, Bruin opened his eyes and focused on Juan. He spotted the way the slender man nibbled his bottom lip. His shoulders betrayed his tension, having hunched a little.

"Juan," Bruin started in a whisper he hoped carried to his human. When his mate blinked and focused his beautiful brown eyes on him, he continued, "Are you comfortable telling me why you're afraid of sex?" A thought entered his mind, and he just knew the blood drained from his face. "Were you—" Bruin paused, swallowed hard, and tried again. "Were you—" Still, he couldn't finish.

Juan's eyes widened, and he quickly shook his head. "No," he denied. While he lowered his hand from Bruin's face, he gripped tightly to the one of Bruin's that had been cradling it. "No, nothing like that." Then his brows furrowed as he admitted, "Although Crespin threatened to sell my ass on more than one occasion, he never did it."

"Ah. That's why you ran from me, from my home. Isn't it?"

Nodding again, Juan admitted, "I thought he finally did it."

"Okay." Bruin nodded as relief filled him. "So that's not it. Will you tell me what, then?"

Shrugging, Juan looked distinctly uncomfortable as he admitted, "You're a huge guy as it is, and you're a shifter."

Juan peered down at Bruin's crotch, and Bruin couldn't help it. His body reacted to his mate blatantly checking him out. He shifted in his seat, trying to give his hard dick more room in the tight jeans.

Reaching over with his other hand, Bruin crooked his forefingers under Juan's chin and urged him to meet his gaze. "We would go at your speed, my sprite," he told him. "I'll never hurt you, no matter how aroused I become."

After a glance around, Juan leaned forward and mumbled, "But shifters are always bigger than normal. Right?"

"Typically," Bruin admitted. Searching his mind, he tried to come up with a way to soothe his uncertain love. His words made something stick in his mind. "Are you a virgin, Juan?"

He blurted out the question because just the idea that his mate was untouched caused his musk ox to bellow possessively. His shifter instincts to claim and keep safe surged through him anew. It took every bit of self-control he possessed to keep from hauling his sexy sprite into his arms and holding him safely on his lap.

Juan nodded just once, his cheeks taking on a dark hue as he blushed. "What if I'm no good?"

Unable to control himself any longer, Bruin released Juan's hand. He reached over and slid his arms under his human's thighs and behind his back. His mate squeaked as he lifted him and placed him on his lap.

When Bruin wrapped his arms around Juan, holding him firmly against him, he felt the stiffness in the man's body. "Gods, please forgive my impulsiveness, my sprite," Bruin crooned into his ear as he nuzzled him. "The knowledge that I and I alone will have the pleasure of your body, of hearing your whimpers of pleasure, of your cries of ecstasy as I make your body sing with bliss . . ."

"Juan, are you okay with sitting on Bruin's lap?"

Jerking his head up—and getting his head out of his ass—Bruin focused on the tall man standing over them. His dark eyes were narrowed, and he eyed Bruin critically. He crossed his slender, tanned arms over his chest while frowning at him.

"Um, I—" Juan began, then paused to nibble his lip as he glanced from the man to Bruin and back again. "I-I don't know."

"Do you fear my hold, Juan?" Bruin asked softly, rubbing one hand up and down his sprite's back while keeping the other securely around him. "I'll put you back if you wish it."

Although Bruin would hate to lose the feeling of the intoxicating-bundle in his arms.

"What would you like, Juan?" the stranger asked again. From his scent, Bruin guessed him to be some kind of reptile shifter. He arched one black brow, asking, "If it's bothering your injuries, I'd suggest returning to your cushioned chair."

"Shit," Bruin grumbled. "I didn't even think of that." With a groan, he began shifting his arms so he could return Juan to his own seat. "I'm sorry, my sprite."

Juan's hand on Bruin's wrist caused him to still, but his mate's focus was on the stranger. "It's okay, Eli. Sitting on Bruin's lap doesn't hurt." His voice—and scent—still sounded a little off, so Bruin appreciated it when Juan admitted, "I've never sat on anyone's lap before. Well, not since my dad when I was, like, five or something." His brows were furrowed as he admitted, "Is one guy sitting on the lap of another normal?"

Yuma grinned as he crawled onto a dark-haired human's lap.

That must be his mate.

"Yep," Yuma stated as he got comfortable. "Shifters are

47

touchy-feely, regardless if we're the dominant one in the relationship or not." Then Yuma pointed at the guy whose lap he sat on. "This is my mate, Hunter, by the way." He then pointed at the tall, slender male. "That's Eli. He's our pack doctor, so he was probably asking more because he hovers over his patients."

Arching his brow imperiously, Eli stated, "Of course I take the care of all my patients seriously, Yuma." His eyes narrowed at him. "You of all people should know that."

Yuma sighed as he nodded sagely. "And you're damn good at it, Eli."

Bruin figured there was a story there, but he wasn't going to ask. Instead, he focused on Juan. "So, my sprite," he murmured into his ear. "May I hold you while we chat? Touching you" — he sighed — "it calms my musk ox."

"Is that what you are?" Yuma asked curiously. "A musk ox?" After Bruin nodded, he grinned. "I'm a penguin." He pointed at Eli, then at a slender black male who remained seated on a cushion on the ground beside the chair Eli had risen from. "Eli is a python, and Sam is a wolf and Eli's mate." Continuing to smile, he cocked his head. "I would love to see your ox. I've never seen one before."

"You an ox, Bruin?" Rueben asked as he returned. He held a glass of wine in each hand, and he grinned as he took in their positions. "Aww, getting comfy. Awesome."

Rueben held out their drinks, and Bruin took his on instinct. Watching Juan do the same, he wondered if he was acting by rote, too. He didn't ask because his mate seemed a little uncomfortable.

Obviously out of his comfort zone.

Glancing between them and Yuma, Rueben grinned. "That looks like a good idea." He plopped onto the chair Juan had previously been using. "Come here, babe."

Then Rueben gripped Lamar's waist and hauled him onto his lap, almost spilling the man's wine in the process. Lamar sighed deeply, his expression aggrieved. Then he handed Rueben the beer he carried and settled against his chest.

While that had been happening, Eli had returned to his seat, and he'd begun absently stroking his mate's head.

"So, what were you talking about?" Rueben asked after taking a sip of his beer. Then his grin returned. "Oh. Seeing an ox." He turned to Yuma. "Isn't Sam's Texas longhorn bull similar to an ox?"

"Uh, sort of," Yuma replied slowly.

At the same time, Adam—who was sitting on a large lounge chair that he shared with Noah—claimed, "Not really."

"I'm a musk ox," Bruin cut in. "They're very different than what you're thinking of." As Rueben's brows shot up and his lips formed an *oh* of surprise, Bruin dipped his head and whispered to Juan, "I thought Yuma said Sam is a wolf shifter."

He definitely smelled like a canine.

"Rueben means the other Sam," Juan murmured back. "You remember the guy with the scar that arrived at your neighborhood yesterday?"

Bruin nodded absently. "Oh, right. I didn't get everyone's names."

Juan smiled in sympathy. "There's a lot of them."

"That there is."

"So, a musk ox," Adam commented. "Is all your family musk ox?"

"Most of us," Bruin told them before taking a sip of his wine. He realized the *getting to know Juan better* time had passed—at least for right then. Fortunately, Bruin got to hold his mate. "My mammy is the alpha of our family. My father, Winston, is the alpha-mate." Listing all his siblings slowly, Bruin told them, "My brother, Warren, is the oldest. He's our head enforcer. My uncle, Ryzer, is our beta. Then I have two other brothers, both younger, and a younger sister. She's an enforcer, too." Chuckling, Bruin explained, "Warren found his fated mate a couple of decades ago, and I have a couple of nephews and a niece from them." Pegging Juan with an adoring look, Bruin claimed, "Guess my mammy's kids are finding their fated mates in the order of their births. Luke is probably excited that I found you, since it means he'll be next."

"He's the nurse, right?" Eli cut in.

"Right."

Eli hummed. "I'd like to compare notes with him some time." His gaze landed on Juan. "He did an excellent job."

"Luke is good at what he does," Bruin confirmed. Then, clearing his throat, he focused on Juan. "My youngest brother, Link, works for the Shifter Council's cyber division. May I have your permission to give Crespin's information to him? That way, the council enforcers have a better chance of tracking him down?"

Juan scent immediately turned to fear at the mention of his half-brother.

Damn.

Rubbing over Juan's side lightly, Bruin murmured, "I don't bring him up to upset you, my sprite." He pecked a kiss to Juan's temple. "I only wish to help catch him as swiftly as possible, so he'll no longer be a threat."

Letting out a deep sigh, Juan nodded slowly. "Yeah. Okay." Then he took a healthy sip of his wine before sharing as many facts as he could about Crespin. Before Bruin could ask any questions, Juan added, "You might want to consider looking into Alpha Alberto, too. He led the roll we escaped from, and he's . . . not a good alpha." Cocking his head, Juan revealed, "I can't imagine he was too pleased to have one of his baby-makers being taken away from him." His cheeks darkened as he added, "Or one of his cleaning slaves."

"Slaves? Plural?" Adam leaned forward, scowling. A growl entered his voice. "Were there others that were treated as you were?"

Juan quickly shook his head. "No. Not like you're thinking," he quickly countered. "Everyone other than the inner circle had to do all the menial chores . . . unless they were pregnant. Some of the women were happy to pop out babies so they could sit around on their asses."

"Sit on their asses?" Bruin murmured in confusion. "How could they be sitting on their asses if they're chasing a bunch of cubs?"

"Cubs were raised by the community, for the most part," Juan told him. "Maria worked hard to be an exception."

Bruin nodded absently, thinking about the shit life his poor mate had had for so long. "I'm glad you came to me," he whispered, nuzzling his temple. "I can't wait to spoil you rotten, so you can sit on your ass all day and never do anything you don't want to do again."

To Bruin's pleasure, Juan chuckled softly. "I'm not sure I'd like that," his sprite admitted. "Um, can I ask a question?"

"You may ask me anything," Bruin told him.

"Would you, um, would you be interested in getting some food, maybe a bottle of wine, then going to my room with me?" Bruin's shock must have shown on his face, for Juan's cheeks turned a pleasing shade of pink even as he rushed on, "Not for sex. I'm not ready for that, but I'm ready for some alone time with you now . . . please."

Bruin drained the last of his wine. As he set the glass aside, he rumbled, "I would love to do that with you, Juan."

CHAPTER EIGHT

Lying on his bed, his eyes closed and his throbbing erection in his hand, Bruin groaned deeply. He slowly stroked himself, recalling the gloriously sweet interaction he'd enjoyed with Juan the prior evening. His mate had felt fantastic in his arms.

Once they'd made it to the room, Bruin and Juan had sat at the table and eaten the food they'd brought. At first, his mate had been stiff and uncertain. It might have been the wine, but he'd slowly relaxed.

Bruin still couldn't believe Juan's whispered confession.

"I've never kissed anyone before."

Just hearing that admission, Bruin had needed to bite back a possessive growl. Instead, he'd asked, "Would you like to experience your first kiss, Juan?" He couldn't have helped his husky voice even if he'd tried. "I would very much like to give it to you." Upon seeing Juan's uncertainty, Bruin had offered, "How about I sit against the headboard, you straddle my lap, and we go at your speed." Never had he wanted something so much than his desire to hold Juan in his arms again. "And if you're only comfortable with talking, that's fine, too."

Recalling the way Juan had nibbled his bottom lip, Bruin felt a bead of pre-cum ooze from his jutting shaft. He'd wanted to use his thumb to tug the abused flesh away from Juan's teeth. Then Bruin wanted to suckle it into his own mouth.

Bruin hadn't. Instead, he'd waited ever-so-patiently for Juan's response. When his little sprite had agreed, he'd damn near leaped out of his seat. He'd managed to control himself, though.

Rising with barely leashed excitement, Bruin headed toward the bed. He ignored all his ideas of the other things he could do with his mate on the mattress. Instead, as promised, he'd sat down, positioning his back against the headboard.

Then, Bruin had waited with more patience than he'd realized he had.

Recalling how his patience had been rewarded, with Juan finally crawling onto his lap, Bruin felt his cock twitch in his grip. He remembered placing his hands lightly on his human's slender hips, how his frame felt under his palms, and a bead of pre-cum oozed from his dick. Even just the memory of the weight of Juan's palms on his chest made his balls ache.

Every little action his human made caused Bruin's body to cry out for action, for relief.

Controlling his impulses had been brutal, but Bruin had done it. It had been well worth it, too. Juan had leaned forward and placed his lips a hairsbreadth from Bruin's own.

Taking that as permission, Bruin had gently moved his right hand into Juan's black hair, pushing the long strands away from his forehead. As he'd peered into Juan's dark eyes, his lust had soared. Then Bruin had slowly closed the distance between them. Keeping his hold gentle, Bruin had pressed his lips to Juan's.

Recalling the feel of Juan's lips against his own, Bruin tightened his hold on his cock. He remembered the slide of his flesh against his own, the tentative feel of it, and his balls rolled in his sack. Reaching back, he tugged lightly on them, hoping to delay his release.

Except, then Bruin remembered the flavor of his mate when he'd opened for him. He'd tasted the wine, traces of the food they'd eaten, and under that, something sweet and masculine that was all Juan's own. Needing more, Bruin had lapped along Juan's tongue, touching and teasing.

To Bruin's heady pleasure, Juan had responded by slowly beginning to do a little exploring of his own.

Bruin moaned as he recalled Juan's appendage gliding against this own. His dick jerked and throbbed, but he kept his jacking slow. His breathing began to speed up, and as he remembered the way Juan had started to roll his hips, giving in to instinct he probably didn't recognize, Bruin's balls began to pull tight.

When the memory of Juan whining into his mouth just as the delicious scent of his cum hit Bruin's nostrils tracked through his mind, just as he'd done in that hotel room, he erupted. Groaning deeply, he unloaded. His balls forced burst after burst of seed from his jerking, aching erection.

Unlike in the hotel room, instead of being trapped in his tight jeans, Bruin's seed splattered over his stomach. He continued to work his dick, extending his pleasure as he recalled the blissful look of ecstasy on his mate's face. His sweet new lover had arched his body, tipped his head back, and cried his pleasure.

Of course, how Juan had reacted afterward had doused Bruin's pleasure a little. His mate had tensed, giving Bruin a head's up of his intentions. When Juan attempted to scramble off his lap, Bruin had wrapped his arms around him and held him close while crooning and shushing him.

When Juan had finally stopped struggling, Bruin whispered, "You are so beautiful in your passion, Juan." He'd pressed a light kiss to his neck, just below his ear, and admitted, "I'm so honored, so humbled to have been able to share this moment with you."

For a long moment, Juan remained silent. At least he'd stopped trying to pull free of Bruin's hold. Instead, he relaxed on his chest, panting softly, his warm breath tickling the hairs of his neck and keeping him in a state of semi-arousal.

"Y-You're not upset?"

Confused at the comment, Bruin asked, "Why would I be upset, my sprite?"

Another half dozen heartbeats went by before Juan answered, "Because I came in my pants after just a little kissing." He lifted his head just enough to peer at Bruin through his lashes. "Because I couldn't control myself, and I don't know what I'm doing. I can't even get kissing right."

Bruin had cradled Juan's jaw in his hand and urged him to lift his head a little. After pecking a quick kiss to his beautiful lips, he smiled. "Oh, sprite. Nothing could be further from the truth." Bruin couldn't help but dip his head and whisper into Juan's ear, "Your kiss was so electrifying, made my balls ache so deliciously, that I came, too."

Juan gasped as he straightened. His eyes were wide, and he stared at him in obvious shock. After glancing down between them, Juan met Bruin's gaze again. "Really?" he asked, his tone and scent full of disbelief.

Winking, Bruin asked, "Would you like to see?"

"S-See?" Juan stared at him in shock for a second before whispering, "S-See y-your . . . cock?" He whispered that last word.

Gods, my mate is so innocent.

That was when Bruin realized he needed to stop the teasing. "If you'd like," he offered. "One way or another, I need to clean my groin. I bet you do, too." Bruin indicated the bathroom. "If you want to clean up in the bathroom, I can do the same out here."

There were a number of napkins on the table, after all.

"U-Um, okay." Juan took the out.

When Juan tried to get off of him that time, Bruin let him go. Once Juan had disappeared behind the bathroom door, he'd risen to his feet. He'd grimaced at the feel of the already cooling semen and made his way to the table to clean up.

Bruin had finished wiping himself up as best as he could

and had returned to the bed with a fresh bottle of white wine and a pair of glasses by the time a still-blushing Juan had exited the bathroom. Smiling at his young lover, he'd patted the bed with one hand while holding up a glass of wine with the other.

"Please," Bruin had urged. "Join me. We'll sit, drink, and talk." When Juan had hesitated, he'd added, "Nothing else will happen this night unless you initiate it."

After a few more seconds of clear indecision, Juan had joined him on the bed.

True to his word, Bruin had remained a gentleman, doing little more than holding Juan's hand as they'd shared bits and pieces about themselves.

Hearing the thud of his front door yanked Bruin out of his memories. He pushed to a sitting position as he grabbed a few tissues from the box on the nightstand beside his bed. As he began cleaning himself up, he heard Luke call out to him.

Bruin shook his head as he replied, "I'm about to get into the shower." Unable to resist, he called, "What the fuck are you doing here again? Don't you work?"

Luke had laughed, the sound growing louder as his footsteps tromped up the stairs. "Getting you mated off *is* work, big brother."

Rolling his eyes, Bruin headed into his ensuite.

Ten minutes later, Bruin returned to his bedroom. He spotted Luke sitting in one of his parlor chairs. There were two of them before a small round table. Along the wall to the table's right, Bruin had a coffee maker that used individual pods. Every morning, he would make himself a cup and sit there, relaxing, as he mentally cataloged his plans for the day.

Bruin had the same set-up outside on his personal deck for use on nice mornings, and he couldn't wait until he could share the ritual with his mate.

Does Juan like coffee? Is he a morning person? What if he wants to travel with Kontra?

Bruin grimaced at that last thought. He couldn't imagine not having the support of his family. His family had always had his back.

Needing answers to all those things, Bruin headed toward his closet to get ready for his date, pointedly ignoring his nosey brother, who still hadn't bothered to look up from his phone.

Before Bruin had finished opening the door, Luke stated, "I already got your outfit out. It's on the bed."

Frowning at the medium–blue jeans and pale purple polo shirt spread across the bed — Bruin had purposefully ignored them — he crossed his arms over his chest. He disregarded the way the move made his towel shift a bit. Flashing Luke if it fell was the least of his concerns.

"Why are you trying to dress me for my date?"

Luke scoffed, finally pulling his gaze away from his phone to focus on him. "Because if it's not for work, your fashion sense sucks," he told him with a smirk. Waving at the clothes, he ordered, "Go on. Put them on." Then Luke frowned at him. "How come you didn't trim your goatee this morning? It's too long." Shaking his head, he stood and pointed at the bathroom. "Take care of that first."

"Oh, for the love of —" Bruin grumbled before snapping his mouth shut and growling under his breath. Maybe having the support of his family was overrated. "Why is my goatee too long all of a sudden?"

Rolling his eyes, Luke shook his head. "Did you forget? I bandaged up your mate. It's only been three days since you removed him from that hell." When Bruin just stared at Luke, his brother gaped. "Are you serious?" Luke threw up his arms in exasperation before stating, "Your mate's skin is soft and smooth, too thin even, due to being malnourished by his asshole half-brother."

Bruin had shared everything he'd learned about his mate's

past—within reason—with his family at brunch that morning . . . and he still wasn't following.

"Good grief," Luke muttered, resting his hands over his face. His voice was muffled when he added, "You could damage the skin of his thighs or groin or what-the-fuck-ever if you go down on him in his condition."

Gaping, Bruin spun and hurried to the bathroom to trim his facial hair. No way would he hurt his mate, even by mistake, should he get the chance to explore his man.

Okay. Maybe I do still appreciate my brother's nosiness.

CHAPTER NINE

"These are beautiful," Juan murmured as he peered around the park. "What are they?"

"These are called red dogwoods," Bruin told him, a smile in his voice. "They're flowering right now, and yes, I agree." Then he winked. "Although, not as gorgeous as you, my sprite."

Juan felt his neck heat a little, and he fought to keep the blush from reaching his cheeks. "Um, why do you call me sprite?" He asked what he'd been wondering since he'd met the man.

Bruin hummed as they walked hand in hand through the park. "You remind me of a gorgeous pixie," he admitted. "Slender, toned, with smooth skin and gorgeous dark hair." Bruin lifted his free hand to touch the long hair that flopped into Juan's eyes and around his head. Bruin brushed a few strands behind his ears. "Even with all those bruises and welts, I found you to be a stunning vision." Wincing, Bruin admitted, "I'll admit it makes me feel a little uncomfortable to admit that, even when you were battered and bloodied, I was turned on."

Gaping, Juan froze as he stared up at Bruin. "Me being injured turned you on?"

When Juan tried to tug his hand free, Bruin didn't let him go. Instead, he reeled him in and wrapped his free arm around his waist. "No," Bruin stated firmly. "That's not what I meant." Juan stopped fighting, and Bruin continued, "Why do you think I was uncomfortable?"

Juan thought about that for a moment. "Th-Then why?"

"Your natural scent and the smell of your blood permeated the room," Bruin told him softly. Dipping his head, he touched his nose to Juan's ear. As he spoke, his warm puffs of breath caused a wave of tingles to erupt down his neck. "Your natural aroma called to me on an instinctual level, making it difficult to control my body's reactions." Sighing, Bruin nuzzled while whispering, "You're just so damn perfect, Juan."

Having never been called perfect before, Juan wrapped his arms around Bruin and clung to him. He didn't think it was even remotely true, but he liked the idea of it. Feeling Bruin's answering embrace as well as the way he teased his fingertips along the knobs of his spine, even through his coat, Juan sank into the much larger man's embrace.

After who knew how long, Bruin whispered into his ear, "Shall we finish our walk? There's a gorgeous gazebo in the middle of the park." After a lick and nip to Juan's earlobe, he lifted his head and gazed down at him, adoration filling his dark eyes. "I'd love to show it to you. Maybe kiss you as we stand inside it, the blooming red dogwoods all around us."

Excitement filling him, Juan nodded eagerly. He'd never been on a date before, but so far, Bruin had taken him on a fantastic one. As they started walking again, Bruin keeping an arm firmly around his waist, Juan couldn't help but smile happily.

Bruin had picked him up at his hotel room, where a couple of the guys had hazed him a little, asking for their itinerary, threatening him to keep Juan safe, and laying out dire consequences if anything happened to him. His date had taken it in good stride before leading him from the hotel, hand in hand. They'd strolled down the walk to a nice restaurant.

After their meal, which Bruin had hurried them through with the promise of a surprise, they'd walked out of the restaurant, and Juan had spotted the horse-drawn carriage waiting up the street. He'd been so excited just to pet the horse. Then, to his shock, Bruin revealed it had been waiting for *them*.

Bruin had helped him into the carriage, and they'd been driven to the park. When they'd departed, Juan had petted the horse again, even giving it a treat that the driver had provided.

As they continued their stroll through the park, Bruin commented, "You sure seemed taken with the horse."

Juan smiled up at Bruin for an instant before continuing to peer around the exquisitely landscaped park. Even the Halloween decorations dotted about were done with exceptional taste. "I've always thought they were stunning creatures," he admitted with a snicker. "I used to watch old black and white westerns just to admire the horses."

"Do you want one?"

Sucking in a harsh breath, Juan thought about that. He shrugged one shoulder, trying to buy time. Was there a right answer to the question?

Bruin poked his side a little, getting his attention. "You do, don't you." His smile appeared disarming. "Do you remember me telling you I was a blacksmith a long time ago?" With a wink, Bruin continued, "I could teach you how to ride. That'd be a fun thing to do together."

Figuring they needed to discuss it, Juan asked, "I suppose you expect me to move in with you." He knew how mates worked, after all. "To stay here with you?"

Turning, Bruin took both of Juan's hands in his own. "You're only partially right," he murmured, his brows furrowing. "While I *would* prefer to stay with my family, I'll understand if you need time to accept that." Squeezing his hands, Bruin continued, "You've been through a lot, and I would never force you. We'll have centuries together, so if you want to travel with your family, I'll petition Kontra to go with him." Then he shrugged one shoulder and offered, "Or if you're willing to stay in my herd's community, we could travel in a few decades when I need to remake my identity. The choice is yours."

Juan stared up at Bruin, reading the sincerity on his features. His big, strong lover — *gods, I have a lover* — would put Juan's desires first.

It was a heady realization.

It also made him understand something else.

"I—"

"Should have run far, far away," a voice snarled — a voice Juan knew all too well. "Good for me you ain't too smart."

Cringing and hunching into Bruin, Juan turned to look at the speaker. "Crespin," he whispered. Seeing his half-brother's cruel smile, he shivered. "W-What—" Juan cut himself off, already knowing the answer.

"So you're the asshole half-brother," Bruin rumbled, his voice so deep it vibrated in his chest. "Guess I should do the right thing and call the enforcers so Juan and I can collect restitution from you."

As Bruin spoke, he pulled his phone off of his belt. He kept his other arm firmly wrapped around Juan, which he appreciated.

Crespin sneered. "Restitution? What nonsense are you spewing?" He pointed at Juan, a cold smile curving his lips. "That's my brother, and he's human. Those laws don't apply to family."

"You attacked a defenseless human without provocation," Bruin countered. "Family or not, that's still illegal."

"I had provocation," Crespin bellowed. "He's keepin' my cubs from me." He pointed at Juan, all vestiges of a mocking façade disappearing behind his rage. "I can do whatever I need to get them back."

"Reports of your unfitness as a parent were submitted to the Shifter Council," Bruin stated, his tone unimpressed. "Even if you managed to discover your cubs' whereabouts, you can't take them or even visit them without clearance from the council, or you'll become a wanted shifter." Then Bruin rolled his eyes, his voice turning patronizing. "Oh, wait. You already *are* a wanted man."

"Who the fuck are you that you care?" Crespin snarled as he stalked forward. "Get lost, or I'll give you a taste of what I gave him."

Bruin growled low in his throat. "If you touch one hair on my mate's head, I will end you." As he spoke, he used his arm around Juan's waist to ease him partway behind him.

"Mate?" Crespin scoffed. "You're gonna take that skinny piece o'shit for a mate?" His smile turned predatory. "I suppose I could let you take my useless, skinny brother off my hands . . . for a price."

"Gods," Bruin snarled. "Do you even listen to yourself?" He lifted his phone while adding, "Because I have several people listening to you as you offer to sell your brother to me."

"Bullshit," Crespin cried . . . right before he began tugging off his clothes. As he undressed, he cackled while saying, "And even if it's true, we'll be long gone before they get here."

At first, Juan didn't get it, assuming Crespin's me and you comment meant him and Crespin. A second after his half-brother began to shift into his armadillo form, several other shifters crept from the darkness. Juan spotted two more armadillos along with a bobcat, a hyena, and a puma.

Bruin growled softly as he pushed his phone into Juan's hands. "Hang onto this," he ordered, flashing a hard smile his way before returning his attention to the advancing shifters. Then, in a pained voice, he pleaded, "And please do your best to stay out of their way, my sprite."

Juan didn't need to be told twice. A second later, he watched in awe as Bruin's body burst from his clothes, expanding and changing, fur growing, a tail sprouting, and horns forming. His jaw sagged open as he took in Bruin's musk ox form.

Yep. Nothing like the oxen I've seen in pictures pulling plows.

The inane thought flitted in and out of Juan's brain as he swept his gaze over Bruin's impressive form. The large beast had to stand almost six feet at his shoulder with long, dark-brown hair that nearly reached the ground. From his massive, curved-horned head to his rump, Juan guessed him to be around nine or so feet. His thick legs ended in sharp-looking cloven hooves.

The hyena and bobcat sprang first.

Bruin completely ignored the cat, pivoting to kick at the darting hyena. While he missed, the move forced the beast to skitter away from him. The bobcat landed directly on Bruin's back, but his mate hardly seemed to notice the small cat trying to bite through his thick coat.

To Juan's surprise, the cat couldn't manage it. Unfortunately, that meant the shifter decided to focus on a different target—him.

With a squeak, Juan leaped to the left. To his shock, he slammed into something hard. He hadn't thought he was that close to a tree.

Juan peered up from his position on the ground and found himself staring into the brown eyes of a different musk ox. He gaped, fear and uncertainty filling him. Then the animal lifted its head and caught the lunging bobcat on its horns. With a swing of his head, he sent the smaller shifter flying.

Seconds later, Bruin's musk ox arrived.

While Juan wasn't certain how, he could tell the difference between them. Maybe it was the look in their eyes. His musk ox stared at him with concern and affection. The other male's gaze appeared more intense and assessing.

"Are you Warren?" Juan blurted out even as he clung to Bruin's huge head.

Why wasn't Bruin fighting anymore?

The musk ox, Warren, nodded once before moving past them. Juan used his hold on his shifter's head to rise to his feet as he asked, "Are you injured?"

Once Juan had found his feet, Bruin shook his head slowly, being careful not to jostle him too badly. Still, he took a couple of minutes to rub his fingers over all the hair he could reach. To his relief, Juan didn't feel any blood, although he did come away with some bobcat saliva.

Gross.

Juan wiped that on his jeans, then grabbed one of Bruin's massive horns. "Where did all these guys come from?" he asked absently as he peered beyond where Warren seemed to be keeping guard over them.

A hyena Juan recognized as Payson had already forced the other hyena to submit. Grimes's lion—another enforcer in Kontra's gang—had the cougar in a hold that said submit or die. The bobcat lay still at the base of the tree where Warren had tossed him.

Finally, Kontra, in human form, made up one of four surrounding the three armadillo shifters. The others were Adam's white tiger, Mutegi's warthog, Vail's wolf, and another musk ox whose identity Juan could only guess at.

Kontra peered Juan's way. "You okay, Juan?"

Juan nodded. "Where did you all come from?" he asked in wonder.

The alpha bear scoffed as he grinned at him. "You and your mate are family," he claimed. "You think we wouldn't stick close to you while these yahoos were still on the loose?" He waved absently at the clearly angry armadillos, but the animals didn't dare attack. "We were tailing you when we spotted Bruin's family doing the same." Kontra winked at the musk ox. "Great minds, my friend. Great minds."

Sighing deeply, Juan couldn't help but smile a little. He finally had family that cared about him for more than how fast he could clean the bathroom. His heart swelled as he realized what he would do to keep that . . . forever.

Shaking Bruin's horn, Juan whispered into his large, hairy ear. "Shift, big guy. I need your arms around me."

Bruin immediately complied.

CHAPTER TEN

To Bruin's surprise, after dressing in clothes borrowed from someone in Kontra's gang, Juan didn't ask to return to his hotel room. Instead, he asked to be taken to Bruin's home. Bruin was more than on board with that, but he had to question his little mate as to why.

"Your family came and saved us from my asshole half-brother," Juan commented, stating the obvious while gripping Bruin's hand. "This is going to sound super selfish, but I want that kind of family for my own."

Feeling Juan's hold on his fingers tighten, Bruin squeezed back encouragingly as he continued to drive his pick-up truck.

"And along with an amazingly kind and supportive family," Juan continued softly. "I get you ... someone sweet, thoughtful, and damn good at setting up dates."

Bruin's heart tripped in his chest as he tried to think of something to say. Juan didn't give him a chance. He kept on talking.

"I know I've been a basket case half the time we've been together, but I have been paying attention." Juan furrowed his brows as his tone turned contemplative. "I've always wanted someone who cared for me as much as my father cared for my mother. I know she didn't return his regard, but I understand fated mates, even if they weren't ones." Lifting his head, Juan smiled at Bruin. "There are plenty of amazing examples in Kontra's gang. I've only been traveling with them for a few months, but those couples" —he sighed, smiling— "those kinds of relationships are what I want." Cocking his head, Juan asked, "Do you think we could fall in love like that? Always supporting each other? Ever faithful? All that romantic bullshit that most humans don't believe in but that the paranormal live by?"

Bruin squeezed Juan's hand. "Abso-fucking-lutely," he stated firmly. Then he cleared his throat. "You said you've only been traveling with them a few months. Did you want to keep traveling with them?"

Juan shook his head. "No."

Glancing Juan's way, Bruin wondered if he should question him further.

With a smile that appeared understanding, Juan murmured, "I was planning on telling you earlier, but Crespin interrupted me." Then he frowned. "What will happen to him?"

Bruin blew out a slow breath as he parked in his garage. Turning to face Juan, he took both of his mate's hands between his own. "I don't want to speculate, but I fear he may be put to death for his crimes," he warned. "He enslaved you, beat you, starved you, and forced a female to mate with him against her will." Bringing one of Juan's hands to his lips, Bruin pressed a light kiss to it before whispering, "I'm sorry, my sprite. His life is not worth your concerns."

With Juan holding Bruin's gaze, he watched his sprite's expression turn sad. "I know. He made his bed, and now he must lie in it." Wincing, he muttered, "Or die in it."

"Exactly," Bruin whispered.

Juan's next smile appeared forced, in Bruin's opinion, when he looked at him again and asked, "Will you take me into the house and fuck me?"

Bruin blinked once, twice, his lips parting with his surprise. "No," he answered gruffly. Juan's shoulders sagged in obvious disappointment, so Bruin quickly cradled his jaw and told him, "I *will*, however, take you into the house, to our bed, and make love to you."

As Bruin watched, Juan swallowed so hard his Adam's apple bobbed. "You will?" His voice came out almost a squeak.

"Mmmm-hmmm," Bruin replied with a serious nod.

"D-Does that mean—" Juan hesitated, clearly struggling.

Bruin waited, trying to be patient. Never would he push his mate, but he wanted to help him ask for what he needed, too. "Talk to me, my sprite," he urged, doing his best to be encouraging. "Anything you want." Lifting one of Juan's hands to his lips again, Bruin brushed a kiss over his knuckles as he purred, "Talk to me, Juan."

In a rush that made the words difficult to understand, Juan blurted out, "Does that mean you'll claim me?"

Bruin sucked in a harsh gasp as lust clouded his thinking. He thought he would have to wait for so very long to hear that request. "I would very much like to claim you, Juan," he whispered, heat coursing through his body as his arousal crested. "If you're certain."

To Bruin's confusion, Juan tugged his hand free. He remained still, watching with bated breath, as Juan cradled his jaw between his palms, sending goose bumps down his neck. His sweet sprite smiled widely at him.

"I appreciate that you're so worried about what I want." Then Juan narrowed his eyes as he gave him a stern frown. "But I'm not a child. I've been taking care of myself as well as Crespin's house for over eight years. I know my own mind." Leaning closer, Juan pecked a kiss to Bruin's lips, the flesh soft and sweet against Bruin's own. He nearly vibrated with the need to cup Juan's jaw, but he was glad he'd resisted when Juan leaned back and purred, "Now. Let's go in, and you will claim me as your mate."

The hairs on Bruin's arms stood on end as shivers racked his spine. That was the first time Juan had initiated their touching, and it instantly caused his cock to throb in his bor-rowed jeans. Good thing the shifter gang always carried extra clothes in their motorcycles, or Bruin would have been in Warren's shirt, blatantly showcasing his excitement.

Pushing aside that random thought, Bruin focused on the here and now and his mate's request.

"Get out of the car, my mate," Bruin ordered gruffly. "It's time for me to eat your ass until you scream from pleasure and come. Then I'm going to slowly open you with my fingers while I suckle and nurse on your dick until you beg me to sink into your body, possessing you from the inside out." As he'd been speaking, Bruin's voice had deepened, growing husky. "Are you ready for that?"

For a few seconds, Juan said nothing, and the fear that he'd said too much grew in Bruin's heart. Then he noticed the flush staining his mate's cheeks and the way he panted. The heavy aroma of arousal permeated the cab of the truck, and it wasn't all his own.

My mate likes my ideas.

"Answer me," Bruin demanded gruffly, turning his head and kissing Juan's palm where it remained on his face. "Tell me you're ready."

"Yes!" Juan gasped out. "Yes, I'm ready."

Bruin pulled away from his mate and leaped from his truck. Sprinting around the vehicle, he reached the door just as it was beginning to open. He tugged it the rest of the way open and reached inside. After confirming Juan's belt was off, Bruin lifted his mate from his seat, eased him from the truck, and used his hip to close the door.

Bridal style, Bruin carried Juan into his home. As he climbed the stairs, he recalled the first time he'd done this. It had only been a few days before, but things had been so dif-ferent then. Juan had been battered, beaten, but not broken.

Time to revel in my mate's resilience and make him mine.

Bypassing the spare suite Bruin had placed Juan in the first time, he carried his mate into his own room. Ever-so-gently, he placed his human on the middle of the bed. Noticing the scent of nerves Juan was trying to hide behind a smile, Bruin gave his mate a slow, lingering kiss, making sweet love to his gorgeous sprite's mouth.

Bruin brought the kiss to an end when pre-cum dampened his fly and his tingling balls threatened pre-mature release. Panting softly, he whispered, "Don't move. I'll take care of everything."

Even as Juan nodded, Bruin opened his nightstand. He grabbed the lube and tossed it onto his bed. Then he made quick work of removing his borrowed clothes.

Once Bruin stood naked before Juan, he spotted the way his sweet mate nibbled his bottom lip. His forever love's nerves flooded the room with a spicy scent that tickled his nose uncomfortably. Needing to remove that smell as swiftly as possible, Bruin set to work distracting his mate.

Bruin first removed Juan's shoes and socks, then took a couple of minutes to massage his lover's feet. When his human's appreciative sighs filled the room, he moved to his jeans. After swiftly removing them, he gave first one calf, then the other, the same treatment.

At the same time, Bruin eased between his legs. He nuzzled the inside of Juan's knees with his lips, licking and sniffing, taking in his scent. As Bruin worked the massage higher, he licked and nibbled at his inner thighs.

When Bruin reached Juan's underwear-covered groin, he noted his sweet mate's straining erection. Drawing on years of self-control, he bypassed the tempting treat. Instead, Bruin gripped Juan's shirt and pushed it up, urging his lover to release his hold on the comforter long enough to strip it from his body.

Bruin took advantage as he tossed the nice shirt off the side of the bed. Levering over Juan, he captured his lover's lips.

After a moment of exploring his mate's succulent mouth, Bruin eased the kiss to an end.

Then Bruin set about doing as he'd promised.

Before Juan could utter a complaint, Bruin eased back down his body. He took several long moments to take his time licking, sucking, and nibbling at his skin, nipples, and the dips of his stomach and hips. When Bruin reached Juan's underwear, he reveled in the way his mate was near-boneless as he maneuvered the fabric from his body.

Bruin tucked his nose against the groove of Juan's hip and inhaled deeply. Groaning, he let the breath out. The heavenly scent of Juan's arousal caused his mouth to water with his desire and his cock to throb.

Ignoring his own need, Bruin cradled Juan's ass cheeks and lifted. He heard his mate's squeak of surprise but pushed ahead with his plans. As soon as Bruin buried his face in his mate's crack and stuck out his tongue, the noises his mate made quickly changed.

With Bruin's tongue swirling around Juan's opening and applying teasing pressure, Juan shuddered and jerked in his hold. His mate's body trembled and twitched while the scent of his arousal thickened in the room. When Bruin pushed his tongue into his mate's heat, his sprite's unique flavor burst across his tongue, and he felt a bead of pre-cum slide across his sensitive cock head. His gut clenched with need, but he continued to work his human, driving his pleasure higher and higher.

Juan's whimpers of pleasure mixed with him crying his name were music to Bruin's ears. When his mate began tugging at his hair, he knew it was time. Easing his tongue from Juan's channel, he lowered his lover's body back to the bed.

Then Bruin swallowed Juan's erection to the root. His mate's scream of pleasure echoed in his ears even as his sprite's release hit the back of his throat. Easing off just a little,

Bruin grabbed the lube even as he rolled his human's next spurt across his tongue, relishing the surprising flavor of his mate's seed, which was slightly sweet.

While continuing to suckle and enjoy Juan's flavor, Bruin poured slick onto his fingers. He quickly eased in one finger just as Juan stopped spurting. After a few initial thrusts, he eased a second finger in while never stopping his nursing of Juan's dick.

Bruin immediately felt Juan begin to tense, so he teased over his mate's prostate each time he eased his fingers in and out of his lover's body.

Juan moaned as he began shifting his limbs restlessly on the comforter. Just as Bruin had promised, his beautiful sprite began to whimper and urge him on, begging for more. Giving it to him, Bruin teased over his prostate with each pass so he could slip a third finger inside his mate.

"B-Bruin, please," Juan whispered. "I-I-I n-need. I—"

Finally, Bruin popped off Juan's cock. "I know what you need."

Bruin carefully pulled his fingers free of Juan's body, grimacing upon hearing the man's whimpers. They couldn't be helped. As he levered over his mate's body, he gripped his dick, smearing it with the remaining slick.

Hovering over Juan, Bruin pecked a kiss to his mate's lips before asking, "Are you ready to be mine, my sprite?" At the same time, he kissed his cock head to Juan's prepared hole. "Can we be together for eternity?"

"Yes, Bruin," Juan whispered, blinking to clear his lust-fogged eyes. Grinning up at him, he wrapped his arms around Bruin's shoulders. "I'm ready to be yours . . . forever."

Bruin groaned as he pressed into his forever love, urging him to push out. Hearing the hitch in Juan's voice and seeing the pinch of his lips, he paused with his dick halfway in his mate. "B-Breathe, my sprite," he mumbled, doing his best to stay still. "B-Breathe and relax, Juan."

Juan crunched up and pressed a kiss to his lips. "I'm re-laxed," he countered. "Now do it." Then he planted his feet and rocked his hips, causing Bruin's erection to sink even deeper. At the same time, Juan ordered, "Claim me."

Never one to second-guess his strong-willed human's orders, Bruin prepared to do exactly as Juan requested. Wrapping his arms around his lover, he clutched his sprite close against him. Then he obeyed, rocking into him over and over, driving them both out of their minds before claiming Juan and making his sprite his own for all eternity.

ABOUT THE AUTHOR

Charlie started writing fantasy when she was eight, and after stumbling onto her first erotic romance at age nineteen, she realized her true calling. She now focuses on writing gay erotic romance, normally of the paranormal variety, with heroes of all kinds. With the help and support of her husband, Charlie finally fulfilled one of her life-long goals . . . move to acreage with her horses. You can often find her curled up with her laptop and a cup of tea or glass of wine, creating her next adventure. Charlie enjoys exploring the mountains of her new Oregon home on horseback, 4-wheeler, or motorcycle.

She can be reached at ch.richards2010@yahoo.com
Or visit her at www.charlie-richards.com